THE HOLY
TORTILLA
and a
Pot of Beans

Other books by Carmen Tafolla:

Poetry:

Get Your Tortillas Together

Curandera

Sonnets to Human Beings & Other Selected Works

Sonnets and Salsa

Non-Fiction:

To Split a Human: Mitos, Machos y la Mujer Chicana

Recognizing the Silent Monster: Racism in the 90s

Tamales, Comadres, & the Meaning of Civilization

For Children:

Baby Coyote and the Old Woman / El coyotito y la viejita

*That's Not Fair! Emma Tenayuca's Struggle for Justice /
¡No Es Justo! La lucha de Emma Tenayuca por la justicia*

The Dog Who Wanted to Be a Tiger

What Can You DO With a Rebozo?

What Can You DO With a Paleta?

Fiesta Babies

THE HOLY
TORTILLA
and a
Pot of Beans

a feast of short fiction by

Carmen Tafolla

WingsPress
San Antonio, Texas

The Holy Tortilla and a Pot of Beans © 2008 by Carmen Tafolla

Cover art © 2008 by Thelma Muraida

First Edition: 2008
First Edition, Second Corrected Printing: 2010
Third Printing: 2015

ISBN: 978-0-916727-49-9
ePub ISBN: 978-1-60940-036-1
Kindle ISBN: 978-1-60940-037-8
Library PDF ISBN: 978-1-60940-038-5

Wings Press
627 E. Guenther
San Antonio, Texas 78210
Phone/fax: (210) 271-7805

On-line catalogue and ordering:
www.wingspress.com
All Wings Press titles are distributed to the trade by
Independent Publishers Group
www.ipgbook.com

Library of Congress Cataloging-in-Publication Data:

Tafolla, Carmen, 1951-
  The holy tortilla and a pot of beans : a feast of short fiction / by Carmen Tafolla.
-- 1st ed.
     p. cm.
  ISBN-13: 978-0-916727-49-9 (alk. paper)
  ISBN-10: 0-916727-49-1 (alk. paper)
  1. Mexican Americans--Fiction. 2. Hispanic Americans--Fiction. I. Title.
PS3570.A255H66 2008
813'.54--dc22
                          2008015842

*To you, the reader, mi gente, and to all the magic,
hope, cariño, and scary stuff that lies beneath your skin,
inside your chest, and rooted in your alma.*

Contents

Our Daily
Tortilla

Chencho's Cow

It all began when Chencho's cow kicked over a pot of beans. The very pot of beans that Chencho had so painstakingly prepared the night before for the Amados' baby's celebration. He'd selected the beans with care, cooked them on a low fire for hours, added salt, chile, and bacon, then put in the *tomate, cilantro,* onions, and more bacon near the end. Then, of course, the crowning touch – a can of beer – to make them *frijoles borrachos,* little drunk beans that he would ladle up into small cups. People downed them like chocolate syrup, only better, not leaving even a teaspoonful of juice at the bottom, and always going back for more.

It was a special occasion. Elena and Javier Amado had given birth to a round-cheeked boy whom they named Carlos Javier, after both their fathers; and Chencho, their neighbor, was invited to the gathering at the house after the baptism. In fact, he was on his way to the party with the aromatic pot of beans cradled in potholders when he heard the cow "moo" loudly and decided to make certain she still had enough water to last until he returned.

It was for being in a rush (as problems usually are) that he laid the pot down so close to her, thinking just to run the hose a minute and continue on his way. But the smell of those delicious drunk beans must have made the cow more energetic than usual, and when Chencho turned around to pick up the hose, she followed him, kicking over the beans and all their *jugo* onto the thirsty dirt.

Chencho found himself in a true quandary. He wanted to go to the party, but he wanted to take a pot of beans with him. He thought about making up some quick *papa con huevo,* or squeezing some juice for *aguas frescas* into a large, *galón* bottle, but that wasn't what he wanted to take. He wanted to take a pot of beans. Worse than that (and the truth had to be told), he wanted to take *that* pot of beans – the very pot he had made with young Carlos Javier Amado in mind, and that now lay flavoring the red, sandy dirt.

He stared at it, he *wished* it back into the pot, he even thought about scooping up what he could, but one look at the cow (and one smell) changed his mind. There was simply nothing that could be done.

The party was as pleasurable as imagined. The townspeople were happy to congratulate (and toast) the young child. Everyone understood about the beans, and they all agreed with Chencho that it was a terrible shame. Chencho took his accordion and played for the party, and even promised the young couple a replacement pot of beans for the next Sunday round of visitors. Everyone went home feeling good. Everyone except Chencho.

Every day for a week, he would go out into the barn and stare at the floor, jealously remembering that pot of beans. It got to the point where he began to neglect his fields, and one day, he even shouted angrily at his cow. He apologized to her, but still it bothered him – it even bothered him that it bothered him.

One morning, as Chencho was standing in the barn heaving one of his now-customary sighs, someone said, "It doesn't have to happen that way, y'know." Behind him stood an *avena*-faced Anglo, a man dressed formally and all in black, like one of those *Protestante* ministers, hat coolly in hand. The man pointed to where Chencho's beans had by now (Chencho was sure) fertilized and strengthened the ground with their nutrients. "Such a waste and all for no necessary reason," said the stranger.

Chencho was startled a bit and also a little embarrassed, as if someone had caught him without his clothes on. "My beans?" Chencho verified, his discomfort not permitting any more eloquent a response than that. "Mm-hm," the stranger nodded, and looked coolly at the rim of his hat.

"You heard about my beans?" Chencho asked.

"Mm-hm."

A moment of silence passed between them, their wandering eyes missing each other's intentionally.

"Hate to see you feelin' so bad, m'friend."

Funny the way the gringos, especially this kind that traveled through and appeared from nowhere, leaving also into nowhere, liked to call you "my friend," though they had never laid eyes on you before and didn't even know your name. He felt so irritated and embarrassed that this stranger should know so much about him.

He tried to retract from that intimacy, awkwardly, but in a definite retreat.

"I'm alright." His embarrassment and the mutual silence belied his attempt. Chencho took a few steps to the side, and then – thinking better – to the front. The gringo looked away politely.

"It's just that they were for a very special fiesta . . . in the home of my young neighbors . . . the baby boy was named after his two grandfathers – very fine men, very well-respected. . . . I'd wanted to give them. . . ." Chencho realized he was rambling and stopped.

"Sure, nothin' the matter with that. Just bein' proper. Anyone could understand that." Chencho relaxed. The man continued, cautiously. "All the same, it do prove a bother, given everythin'." Chencho's brows came together as he studied the talkative gringo. "An' the most bothersome part comes down to just one thing –" Chencho was caught. No one had talked to him about it with such concern since the day after the party, as if everyone else had forgotten or worn out the interesting part of it, and Chencho had only himself to talk it over with. "Just one thing, m'friend, at the root of it all – causing you this heartache. . . ." The gringo held the moment, letting Chencho hunger for an answer. "Passion! Jus' plain passion!"

¡Gringo entremetido! Chencho thought. I knew he was sticking too far into my private feelings!

"Now don't go backin' off, m'friend. This is a problem common to the majority of human bein's that inhabit this planet! An' to darn near all of the animals! Why that cow of yours just got so excited by the smell o' those beans that she jus' had to kick up her heels an' dance across the floor behind you, kickin' over those special beans o'yours. You'd a thought she would've stepped over logically, or waited till you got the water filled an' was out o'the way, but she jus' got so filled up with passion." Chencho was listening again. "Passion's what did it! Why, people go near all their lives getting' their feelings hurt or broodin' over things, cause o' the trouble that passion causes 'em. . . ."

⋯⟡⋯

By the time he cleared the dishes off the lunch table, Chencho was feelin' pretty good. The gringo had brought in a couple of bottles of elixir from behind the panels of his truck (to cleanse the body after eating, he said) and Chencho was feeling more relaxed than he'd been in a week, with the drone of the gringo's voice putting him just a little (but not too much) to sleep. It never occurred to him to ask what could be done about it; it just somehow made more sense for this whole incident to have had some reason. But the gringo was on his way to some special road. "If only they didn't have their hearts gettin' in the way all o' the time, so much could be accomplished. . . ."

—➤●◄—

Chencho didn't remember having really thought about it a lot. In fact, he didn't really remember how it all happened. But his cow seemed to be doing fine, and the gringo reassured him that she was actually doing better than she ever had before. Even the scar where her heart had been taken out didn't seem to bother her. And the gringo was sure to point out that she would never again moo at him crossly when Chencho was late to feed or milk her. In fact, she would never again moo at him at all. There was simply no reason to do so.

There was still the matter of Chencho staring at the spot in the barn and savoring not only the memory of the beans, but of the whole *celebración* as he had envisioned it, but the gringo had an idea that he said would take care of that, too. It wasn't that Chencho had so much confidence in the gringo – he was a curious sort that did too much talking and not enough waiting – but it was just that the man had a way of getting him to agree without asking his opinion.

"Passion! M'friend, without our hearts, we could get so much more done, and with so much less pain. Now, I wouldn't recommend this to ya' if I didn't happen to have seen it work so many times. If we weren't so emotional, we'd have lots more space for being logical. Why the proof o' that's women, ain't it? Get so emotional they don't have an ounce o' logic in'm. Now that's one that a good man like you can really understand, can't ya'?" he said, laughing and elbowing Chencho. Chenco didn't, but he laughed anyway, from the mouth outwards, as they say in Spanish, but enough to keep from looking too unmasculine to the gringo.

This time, Chencho insisted on taking the night to think about it. He would have put if off much longer, but the gringo said he had appointments to keep in another town and would have to leave this town "sooner that I'd like, m'friend." Chencho talked about it plenty with his neighbors, and some of the things his cousin Nilo said got him so upset that he spent the whole night struggling with his pillow, and by morning was ready to give it a try, just to rid himself of this problem. He went out to the barn where the cow was standing, looking very peaceful and unconcerned.

"You'd be considered quite a man to have that kind of calm and strength in every situation."

Chencho turned to look at the gringo, and something about the man's absoluteness, stark black and white against the brown of the barn, made Chencho want to trust him, want to really make his "m'friend" expression a reality. He was a little nervous about the cutting part, but the gringo explained that the reason the wound had healed so rapidly on the cow (in fact, it was not even like a wound at all) was that nothing really biological had been removed, only the emotional mass, the heart itself. And without the bother of this too-emotional muscle in its chest, the body could proceed with even greater health, allowing the brain to take over the functions previously so poorly supervised by the heart.

Maybe it was Marta's grandfather, the one with the weak heart, that did it first, after Chencho. Or maybe it was *la rica,* the one who was always so scared of someone stealing the blue tile birdbath that she'd bought in Mexico and placed so precisely in the perfect shady spot in her garden. No one seemed to remember how it had all happened, but they did recall that there were long lines in front of Chencho's house and that everyone went in very envious and excited, admiring how well Chencho was doing. And when they came out, they looked very happy, or maybe it was strong, or in control, they weren't certain which. At any rate, by the time three suns had set, there wasn't a normal-brained person over the age of ten that hadn't had their heart removed by the kind gringo who brought them the science of "depassionization," as he called it. Chencho's mother had been one of the last to agree. For three days she ranted and raved (quite passionately, proving the gringo's point) against the whole idea. She said that if God had meant people not to struggle for anything, he would have given women "labor thoughts" instead of labor pains. The strangest thing of all was that the reason she probably gave in and had it done was because of passion itself! She just couldn't stand to see everyone else in such a predicament and her not right in there with them, with her hands in the *masa*, so to speak.

Chencho's mother had made certain, however, before placing herself defiantly in that line, that her retarded niece, Eva, would not be touched. The gringo agreed emphatically, stating that it really wouldn't work well on the mentally unfit or on children under ten because, with as little as they'd accumulated up top, they wouldn't have anything left to lean on.

It wasn't until weeks after the gringo left that they realized something was missing. At first, they thought they were just forgetting things, making a mistake or two, or having a dull day. But the pattern was noticeably repeated. Their thinking no longer seemed as sharp, and the reasons for thinking things out were not known. Many things left a taste of not having been tasted. Chencho discovered that he no longer remembered how to make beans. This was the case with numerous things: they had to look elsewhere to find what had once been inside of them.

Chencho contacted a cousin in a neighboring city and made clear the level of his need. The necessary papers were sent promptly. Chencho would focus all of his attention, following the directions with great care. Each step was outlined elaborately. Cleaning the beans required spreading them on the table, removing the stones, removing the beans that were shriveled and dried up, eliminating those that had an unnatural dark color that looked burnt and hardened, while leaving those that were dark in the same shade as the dark spots on the light beans. It seemed so complex. He had first learned to clean the beans as a child, but he had not learned with his head. He had learned with his heart, while watching his grandmother do that which had later become integrated into his view of life. Now, it was integrated into nothing more than the piece of paper he studied so thoroughly, stumbling through the applications.

"Wrinkles that come with life, wrinkles from rubbing against other beans, wrinkles from wilting under the sun – all right. Wrinkles of petrified stone – no." He worked at it repeatedly, adding precisely measured amounts of ingredients at precisely timed stages. Chencho found that every time he cooked beans, he needed to follow the written instructions again. It was as if there was some ingredient missing, but he had no idea what to add.

Chencho and the others would sit in the evenings, trying to piece together those things that their hearts could no longer provide. Eva, the retarded thirty-five-year-old, began to play a special role. She was the one they turned to for lessons in how to cuddle babies and how to help the children play. They listened carefully as she and the little children laughed, trying to imitate the sound.

They tried to make lists of what it was they had lost, had had, and had said in those days of the gringo's visit. They tried to piece together old conversations, but, somehow, every conversation had something important missing between the lines. The eight- and nine-year olds were brought in to listen and respond, but even their responses were difficult to comprehend. The teenagers just took notes. Chencho's mother proposed they go over every event and every conversation from the day of the gringo's arrival to the day of his departure. Chencho remembered him climbing into the truck with some salutation, what was it? The children offered possible expressions until the right one was found. "Goodbye, my friend," the gringo had said, as he shoved the roll of worn dollar bills into his pocket. "And then what?" asked Jorge, as the Amados' baby began to cry and the adults turned to stare at him. "The baby wants his bottle," said a bright-eyed seven-year-old.

Chencho thought carefully, and found the information as best he could through his passionless brain. "And then he told me how fortunate we would be – to be able to work longer days in the sun, without feeling upset, and to bring home paychecks of any amount at all, without wanting to cry."

"What?" asked Elena, thoroughly confused, "Without wanting to cry?"

"Yes, that's what he said."

"Is that all?" asked his mother, whom people somehow sensed should be regarded as a leader, although they were not certain why.

"No," said Chencho slowly, "There was something more . . . something he did . . . like that, like what that child just did."

"He laughed?" asked the seven-year-old.

"Yes, that was it. He laughed. He laughed," Chencho verified, "And then he drove off."

In the distance, Chencho's cow could be heard moving around the barn, her bell dangling against the trough as she searched for food, but everyone knew that she would never again bother to moo.

La Santísima María Pilar, the Queen of Mean

María Pilar wasn't the meanest character I ever met. But that's just because the devil made regular appearances in our part of town. I dunno. I tried real hard all through junior high and even ninth grade to be a good Christian. You know, "Do what Christ would do. Feel love in your heart for everyone. We're all brothers." But if María Pilar had been MY brother, I'd have run away from home. There was no feeling in my heart for María Pilar that even LOOKED like love.

I don't know why a person can get that mean. Maybe her name had something to do with it. The María Pilar part was okay. Everybody in my neighborhood was María something – María Luisa, María Encarnación, María Elena. And when a girl's first name wasn't María, it was stuck in someplace else, like in the middle, like Anamaría or Rosamaría. Even one or two of the guys were called José y María or María Guadalupe. María's a pretty popular name where I come from. But it was when her mom got carried away and stuck in the "Holy of Holies" part, La Santísima, that fate must have taken its turn. Or maybe she was just born mean already when she got into this world, so her mom took one look at her and got so scared she tried to wipe away all the meanness with the holiest name she could think of. Whatever. It didn't work.

La Santísima María Pilar was as mean a human being as I'd ever met. Now, I guess the devil don't really count as a human being, and while he did show up a lot in our *barrio* – I told you that, right? – especially on Saturday nights when people were ready for some excitement, and were thinking about all the nasty stuff that had come out in confession – it still didn't carry the same shock level as when you knew a real, real human being that wasn't just being the devil cause that's what he is, but was being mean, mean, mean, like no human being you ever seen. I mean, the devil you kind of expect it from, and it's even kind of fun to hear about it, you know? But with María Pilar, she was too mean for anyone to even have fun talking about it afterward.

Well, the meanest thing she ever did I won't even talk about. Like I said, it's no fun. And if I did, you wouldn't believe me anyway, but I guess it's okay to tell you some of the stuff, like the small stuff, that's the only stuff I care to remember anyway.

Like the time it was her gramma's eightieth birthday and her mother forced her to go, and insisted she should take a present. She went, all dressed up and with a nice package in her hands. We thought, "Well, everybody's got to do SOME things right, no matter how mean they are." But when it came time to open the gift, and her gramma smiled in delight at the pretty Avon perfume bottle, María Pilar said, "Try it on, Gramma."

"*Ay, y pónme a mí también,*" said Pilar's self-centered Tía Julisa. So Doña Chana sprayed it merrily on herself, as Julisa darted into the mist, with "*A mí, a mí,* " cutting off the trajectory of the spray bottle with her large flabby arm.

The group's smiles changed to furrowed brows as Julisa yelled, "*Fuchi!*" The aroma wafting across the room reminded me of the rest room at the old gas station by the train tracks, the one with the door knob missing, no light bulb, and where you always have to hold your nose and step carefully cause there's always toilet paper streamers and little yellow rivers all over the floor.

I'll never forget the look that crept over her gramma's face as she realized what must have gone into the perfume bottle. Julisa ran, but Doña Chana weakly excused herself from the group and didn't return till long after we'd heard the shower water run. When she walked back in, she was pale, and her wet hair was pulled back from her face into a still-dripping bun. Everyone tried to continue with a party, but it didn't feel like it anymore.

Or the time Marisa was getting ready for her *quinceañera* , and had every last detail all ready, including the dress and the rosary and the pink paper flowers for the hall and even the fancy bobby pins decorated with tiny pink roses that she was going to pin in a row down the sides of her long silky hair. "*Me voy a ver bien* cool," she had bragged happily, staring at her tresses in the mirror. But María Pilar got that look on her face that some of us knew too well, and next thing you knew she walked up to Marisa with the scissors and chopped one side of Marisa's hair to boy-length. *Hi-i-i-ijo,* Marisa almost didn't go to her own *quinceañera* party, till her aunt convinced her she could wear her hair (what was left of it) up, in a way that the chop wouldn't show, and still pin the tiny roses in. And it really DID look alright. Kind of.

Anyway, I don't like to talk about María Pilar. Nobody does really. Just one thing keeps sticking in my mind. That time at the Easter picnic - *cascarrones* and *fajitas* and a good time, all the time. Somebody would always bring a baseball and a bat, lotta people would make special plates they only made once a year. And then, as the evening got cool, the best of the feast, the king of the crowd - the *fajitas*. The Gomez brothers usually took turns making the *fajitas*, and this time it was Louie Gomez' turn. "Now you gonna get The World's Best," he boasted.

Pancho Medrano (who was always a big mouth) started teasing Omar about who used the pants in his family. And Louie, who nobody thought of as bossing anything at all started talking like he was such a big boss. His one-year-old came waddling past, with a strong cloud of stink surrounding him. "*Anda cámbiale el pañal al bebe,*"(Go change the baby's diaper) he said to his wife, "*Esa es cosa de mujeres.* Women's stuff." But his wife wasn't near enough to hear him (some of us thought that might have been why he said it.) There were really no *women* women within earshot – only three girls - me, Gracie and María Pilar. But me and Gracie had both hands covered with *aguacate* we were peeling for the guacamole, and we just kind of ignored him. Yeah, everyone knew Louie was just like that - a swelled head kind of, only just acting. A man made of balloon. So big, so big, but then you just prick him once and he flies up in a circle, the hot air all comes out, and nothing's left but a little rubbery piece of color on the grass. But we didn't mind. "*Es su modo,*" people would say, "That's the way he is." We're pretty tolerant like that in my *barrio*, I guess. We just ignored him and kept preparing food, snacking here and there on the first round of *fajitas*.

I guess María Pilar didn't feel so tolerant. She was sitting back, finishing off a big plateful of *fajita* tacos when he said that thing about diapers being women's work. The baby was crying by now. Everyone got quiet when she shot a dirty look at Louie, but she just swooshed up the baby and headed for the house where there was a bed.

"Looking good," Pancho hinted, leaning in from across the grill and setting his sights on one of the *fajitas* that looked almost ready. "*¡Ey!*" Louie slapped his hand away, "Nobody messes with my *fajitas*. The MASTER pulls them off when they're ready." Louie picked up the browned fajita with his tongs and laid it tenderly on the serving plate, where Pancho snapped it up before Louie could finish bragging, "There's ten different ingredients that I marinate 'em in!"

When the baby waddled out five minutes later, he was smelling good again. And a few minutes after, María Pilar came out, quiet. Louie, knowing her reputation for meanness, was nervous at first, but when she didn't say nothin, he started puffing up again, just like that balloon, and went back to bragging. "Bring me the other tray of fajitas," he shouted, *muy mandón*, at his brother Tony, "so you can taste what the world's BEST *fajitas* are like. . . ."

———◆———

It was the biggest tray, the one that came after the first "trial run" that everyone knew was just to *"calentar el orno"* as they say. Now *these* were the prime *fajitas* - when the fire was just right, the first set had already been tested, and the evening was early. So Tony rose from where he was sleepily enjoying his second beer, and headed for the kitchen, and people started to line up, almost unconsciously, with their plates in hand, ready to fill up on hot flour tortillas stuffed with *fajitas, guacamole, y salsa.*

Gracie and I finished the guacamole, wiped our hands and ran for a plate and a place in line. Layer upon layer of juicy little strips of meat were transferred from the dark swirling liquid to the fire. The *fajitas* turned a delicious brown, dripping with a dark marinade that coulda made cardboard taste good! "This is it, man," said Louie, "Line up here and get a taste of heaven! They don't make it no better than this!" he shouted.

Everyone who hadn't filled up on the trial batch filed past Louie's tongs, getting really serious about the eating. And my own teeth were just sinking into the smokey *fajitas*, and feeling their delicious juice drip onto my tongue when Louie paraded his own giant taco in front of us, declaring "Like you never tasted anywhere else - Louie's World Famous *Fajitas*" and took a big bragging bite.

Everyone was having a good time, and Louie, having mouthed the first taco down in nothing flat, started to lay out some more *fajita* strips on the grill for seconds. Little kids were running around, giggling, the *comadres* were laughing in between bites, pop tops were popping, and everyone was enjoying the taste too much to even mind Louie's bragging. "*¡Ay voy!* Just let me get this last layer of *fajitas* on the grill and I'll sit down and join you!" Louie said to his buddies, who were too busy eating to care if he joined them or not. "Even the Best has gotta have a Rest!" he said, as he pulled a few more strips of meat out of the tray and then stared oddly at the bottom of the pan. His brows crawled together and his smile disappeared. He put the tongs down and walked away.

"Hey, Louie! *¿Que te pasa?* Thought you were gonna join us!" said his youngest brother Chale.

"*Ay, Dios mío,*" said Mary Sylvia, Louie's wife, as she looked in the pan. She reached in with the tongs and picked up a well-marinated dirty diaper from the bottom of the giant *fajita* tray.

People stopped chewing. A few discretely emptied mouthfuls into a napkin or hanky, others just blurted stuff out like a rocket. Maria Pilar just sat back smugly, eyebrows raised, saying, "He said it was *cosa de mujeres* to change diapers. Then I guess it's also *cosa de mujeres* to decide where to put the dirty diaper."

The party wrapped up pretty much after that. People made excuses to get on home early, and the ones who had just started to eat when the terrible discovery occurred went home to rummage through their refrigerators for some leftover beans or a can of soup. And neither Louie nor the rest of us felt much like *fajitas* again for a long, long time.

——◆——

Not long after, María Pilar went to live with some cousins in the Valley, somewhere near El Pozito. People relaxed, but still, *fajitas* didn't taste the same. We made *barbacoa de cabeza* or *tamales* instead, or even hot dogs, anything that didn't sit in a marinade. And nobody EVER tells ANYBODY else "Go change the baby's diaper." People here either do it themselves, or just pray someone else will. I guess one good thing did come out of it, though. Neither Louie nor any of the Gomez brothers puff up much anymore, and the guys have all quit saying anything about "Women's work" or "Men's work." Scared, I guess. Still, I miss my *fajitas*. I could understand her being mad at Louie, but why'd she have to mess with the *fajitas*? Mess with our

night, she had a little free time left, and could sign up for that correspondence course for college that she'd always wanted. Cuca and Blanca got the same idea about Mondays, and started a "Mothers' Night Out" child care co-op so they could sew crafts to sell (at the restaurant, of course) for extra money.

"Pretty soon, people were putting up signs on the main highway announcing how many miles to Peñitas and Eat at María's Restaurant, and Stanley James' best friend Carla Zavala decided to start a monthly Peñitas newsletter. And the very first issue was dedicated to 'La Pilar, a distinguished Peñitas community leader and civil rights activist.' Course by the time it came out, Pilar and Tony had already moved to Houston, but still - we knew who had started it all."

"I guess we have you guys in San Antonio to thank, huh? Y'all are the ones who shaped her into what she is today, huh!"

I had *baba* dripping down the sides of my mouth, I'm sure, cause I couldn't even close my mouth to open it again and answer her. I left pretty quickly after that and didn't go back to Chava's again for a LONG while after the cousin left.

It bothered me. Someplace in the center of my stomach. I'd liked it a lot better when I was a young kid and we told the scary stories of the devil late at night. I even began to really appreciate the devil. He was a devil, he looked like a devil, he talked like a devil, he acted like a devil. You knew where he stood!

Yeah, I could really appreciate him. A lot. With somebody like María Pilar, she could do mean stuff, but then she would go off and move somewhere else and marry a Tony, who could actually think he loved her and she would actually do something *nice* once in a while. Well, I'm not so sure about the once in a while. Just about the once. But even the thought of her doing something nice *once* made my head hurt. The way I figure it, that Santísima was just finding a new way to be mean - messing with my mind *and* messing with my *fajitas*.

I just hope she stays in Houston, where it's big enough to lose people, and we can really forget about her. Just the same though, I think I'll check out the Little League rules here and make sure our little girls can play too. Just in case. With someone like La Santísima María Pilar in the world, even the devil isn't safe.

The Holy Tortilla

It was rather plain as a baby. Just a little kernel of corn on a boring stalk in a field with cracked, dry dirt and too many brown-tipped leaves. No one would have ever guessed that it would change forever the history of South Texas.

Right from the very moment the kernel sprouted on the cob, the ear of corn started acting differently. The ear spoke strange things at odd moments, saw things others did not see, turned to face the moon instead of the sun, answered questions that were never asked, and was quiet when it was time to agree with the others. Even the stalk noticed. *"Que rara,"* she thought. "That ear had always acted *muy correcta* before. It's probably just a bug." And behind her back the other stalks began to say the same of her.

Since cornstalks were always intent on serenity, they tried to ignore the oddities now happening in the universe. But they could see clearly that new stars appeared nightly in the skies. New voices were heard whispering through the wind. They were omens, really, but everyone tried not to notice. "It's because of the funny weather," the stalk made excuses weakly, when her tender light green cornsilk began to be streaked with a blood purple.

Then, the stalks near her began to recede, until soon there was a circle, a clear space around her, surrounded by stalks that grew away and then arched back towards her, as if they were bowing. She stayed *calmada*, never one to overreact. The ear, who had a funny intuition about it all, began to grow extra thick shucks around herself for protection, just in case. In case of what, she didn't know. But she sensed inside her a deep hunger for meaning, and her soul secretly shivered at the beauty of her own purple silk.

Other than all of that, though, life was pretty normal. There was a strange story or two that the other stalks passed like gossip between them, hesitantly, on the early summer nights, but through all of it, no one blamed the kernel. No one even really noticed it at all. Not until the day when the *señora* who owned the *molino* came to harvest some of her corn and the ear of corn was cut.

The stalks felt it instantly. Then, suddenly, everything was different.

⎯⎯⦿⎯⎯

The ears were taken to a building and stripped of their shucks. Then they were laid on a rough, cutting board, where the kernels were cut off with a knife and ground in a modern metal thing, not as pretty or efficient as a *metate*, but effective anyway. The fresh and fragrant young kernels went in one end of the metal thing and came out as soft, smoothe *masa* at the other end. The man with rippling arms picked up the spackleware tub from under the spout of the metal thing and carried it to a table where a young girl's dark brown hands scooped the moist *masa* up onto a scale, and from there into a bag.

The small *molino* packaged the *masa* in a clear plastic bag with a twist-tie and a plain white label reading "Eva's Tortillas, Alma Seca, Texas" in black print.

The woman in the faded cotton housedress had just finished listening to a re-run of the *novela, Amor Inocente,* her favorite, on the radio, when she opened the package to start supper. The children were watching TV as the first of the *masa* was patted into a round, pleasant-sounding tortilla and slapped onto the hot *comal.* The TV blared out some strange show where the characters looked like cartoons for children but the jokes were all for adults, and the rude gringo family all talked to each other with *desprecio* and discourtesy as if they only held together from apathy rather than from love. So many of this new kind of cartoon these days, all of her *comadres* had sighed, that left an empty but sour taste in their mouths, a hunger for meaning still in their hearts. When the tortilla hit the comal, the youngest child, a cinnamon-skinned toddler with dancing, gold-brown eyes, left the advantaged position at the front of the living room floor and waddled to the kitchen, asking *"To-ti-lla?"*

"Sí, corazón, this one's for you," said the mother. "Just have another minute's *paciencia."*

But as the steam rose from the hot *comal* and she grabbed anoth-er chunk of *masa* to shape the second tortilla, strange figures began to dance amid the vapors above the toasted corn circle. One by one, the children left the false cartoon to gather around the tortilla and watch.

The woman, too, stopped her patting and left the unfinished second tortilla on the plastic counter, as the whole family began to see shapes their hearts recognized. And then, it happened.

Through the clouds of vapor appeared an earth-skinned woman in a bright red dress, tied with a black Karate belt right above her small, round, pregnant belly. She had a *rebozo*, a Mexican shawl, woven in a blue-green folkloric fabric, draped gracefully around her head and shoulders and down to the ground. Stars began to appear in the green shawl, which moved around her head softly, like the breath of a summer breeze. And rays of sunlight began to shine from behind her, framing her figure.

The woman at the stove dropped her dishcloth as she gasped, "It's the Virgin of Guadalupe!" A crescent moon began to appear below the hem of the red dress, below the Virgin's feet. Then, a young black angel appeared, holding up the crescent moon. The family's eyes were transfixed, their heartbeats slow and loud, and no one even noticed as the baby grabbed the raw *masa* of the unmade second tortilla and began to nibble while shapes danced and moved above the cast-iron *comal*.

The Virgin's image was not *on* the tortilla; it was actually moving and turning *above* the tortilla in a three-dimensional way that looked holographic. The Virgin's hands came together in a motion the woman wanted to recognize, then moved apart and turned, came together again. The Virgin looked down at her hands, or maybe at the tortilla, or maybe, each one of them wondered, "Is *She* looking at *me?*"

It was more than an hour before they stopped watching to tell anyone - or maybe they didn't stop at all. Maybe people just dropped by and joined the audience, but soon the whole *pueblito* of Alma Seca was gathered around the *comal*, which the woman had wisely thought to turn off before the tortilla burned. Yet the tortilla had sat on the *comal* for more than an hour already, she later realized, and never burned. It was, they knew, a miracle.

The vapors rising up from the *comal*, though, never ceased, and became more pearly and filled with light whenever the shapes moved or danced. Projected up on the vapors, appearing as if in a dream, but more clearly, was the image everyone saw and recognized. It was, clearly, the Virgin of Guadalupe, but alive and moving, and, unlike their television set, churning out no re-runs. Also unlike their television set, it made no noise, but kept them somehow involved, interacting.

Instead of their voices being drowned out, their voices seemed to be enhanced, richer, clearer, more harmonious with the images projected above the tortilla. They talked among themselves, and listened to each others' answers, as if they themselves were writing the dialogue to this show.

"What does it mean?" asked the town nurse. "What is she trying to tell us?" And cynics and the faithful alike came to ask the same question, and stare at the daily messages - messages spoken with her hands. Sometimes, roses appeared in the background, sometimes Coca-Cola bottles. Disposable diapers, books, *molcajetes*, basketballs – all took their turn in the pictures. It was better than music videos!

The images were somehow deeper, realer, as if they had five or six dimensions, not just three. People watched, but they also debated, cheered, argued, encouraged their own selves. The pregnant *Virgen* did strange things. Once she set a table with mangos and *fajitas*, guacamole, and fresh-squeezed *limonada*, and draped the table with mesquite leaves, red chiles, and tiny, white Christmas lights. Then, as if something had just ocurred to her, she folded fancy placecards out of notebook paper, left the names blank, and giggled, looking the people straight in the eye.

Another time she sat at a window, stroking a large tabby cat in her lap and looking out, over her shoulder, across a field of – sunflowers? Some said they were bluebonnets, just off the highway south of San Antonio. Others saw the blooming red *tunas* of cactus. Still others swore they smelled sweet orange blossoms, just like the ones in Mamá Locha's backyard in Brownsville. After the cat left, the Virgin turned to face the window and only the back of the recliner was visible, with the outline of her elbows. Was she reading? What was she reading? On the left of the window, tamales began to grow from a native olive tree. On the right, a black man with freckles held a laughing baby in his arms.

And then something else happened. The people who came to see the images above the tortilla left with something extra, something *misterioso*, under their skin. They noticed that they were sleeping better, laughing deeper. Even people in a hurry walked at a slower pace, enjoying the road. They admired the small stubborn blooms, so visible now on what used to be ignored as weeds. They heard the sweet melody of the dancing of butterflies, landing on overgrown sunflowers. Life in Alma Seca began to seem filled with music. Several *viejitos* set themselves up nearby with guitars, and people filing past would hear an old voice singing *con alma* "*No hay que llegar primero, pero hay que saber llega-ar*" or sometimes "Celebrate Good Times, Come On!!" in a Tex-Mex-accented rock dialect.

The family did not resent the constant flow of visitors. Instead they would often go outside and share lunches with them. Sometimes, the visitors brought fajitas and a little portable barbecue grill, and the aromas and sounds made the front yard feel like the Fiesta fairgrounds.

Through it all, the Virgin remained quiet, but active. It's as if no sound was necessary from her mouth. People provided the sounds from inside their own dreams. Early one morning, when many were sleeping on the ground around her, pillowed by each other's snores, a few of the early risers said they saw her wearing a little black vinyl fisherman's cap like Selena's, tuning in a boom box, and singing, *toda* cool, with an invisible microphone in her hands, "Cracklin' Rose, you make me smile!" Chala, who knew Neil Diamond's songs by heart, said the Virgin's swinging shoulders and open mouth movements matched that line exactly, and that she herself couldn't stop singing it all day long.

Lunchtime of that same day, people saw her holographic image walking, really SERIOUSLY walking, in big long strides and some comfortable *chanclas*, arms cocked in right angles, strutting so serious and so real that they moved aside to make room for her between them. When she got closer, a man and a woman appeared beside her in the vapors. She put an arm around each, and they walked together. La Mrs. Henderson, the school cafeteria lady, who'd come on the second day and never left since, said she was sure they were relatives, maybe the Virgin's brother and sister! But then, Mrs. Henderson, sweet as she was, DID always think most Mexicans looked alike anyway.

The neighbor ladies started bringing their laundry baskets, so they could fold their clothes with everyone else, a little closer to the tortilla. And even their husbands joined in folding, and some strangers too. The babies were all happier, because there were people all around to hold them *y chulearles*. No one needed play pens, and even the teenagers smiled more.

But not everyone was happy about the tortilla. Local officials impressed with their job titles began to grumble. Didn't people realize there were more important things in life than a holy tortilla?

The *migra* grumbled too. With so many *devotos*, the I.N.S. guys figured, there had to be some *mojados* around somewhere. People in the U.S. aren't as religious as those in Mexico, they argued. People in Mexico are more religious about everything, even about tortillas. In addition, the story the Immigration and Naturalization Service got was that some woman standing in a cloud of vapors at some *rancho* was making gestures and not talking. That sounded like maybe she didn't speak English and wasn't a U.S. citizen, maybe even some involvement with some illegal substance that was being burned or smoked or inhaled! So they sent some agents to check it out. They didn't think there'd be any disadvantage to sending Silver MEN-dez. He never called himself Silverio anymore and they were sure of his loyalties. "Just another one of us," his supervisor said.

But when they got there, something was different right away. First off, nobody noticed them, nobody mumbled or shifted or high-tailed it out. They were too busy watching the tortilla. Pretty soon, all of the immigration guys were watching the tortilla too, and Silver had somehow worked himself into a front row seat, where he stayed for three days solid.

That's when the sheriff decided he'd better check it out too. Or at least that's what he told people. His wife said he was just looking for an excuse to go see it, like everyone else. Besides, he was always a pushover for a hot tortilla.

People were beginning to hang out big time, but the family still didn't mind. They liked the fact that there was more music, more *viejitos* telling stories, more children playing. The Chicano Studies Scholars that had flown in from Germany were asking families for their *fajitas* recipes, and writing down the *viejitos'* song lyrics. Folks would eat and sing, then kind of recycle in to watch the tortilla again, and it would start all over again. She would move, dip down, swing her shoulders, and someone would ask, "Is She dancing?" Tío Nacho said it was to "Hang on, Sloopy! Sloopy, Hang on!" but his son insisted it was the last lines of Iris' Song from the Goo-Goo Dolls. "Yes! Look at her lips! – 'I just want you to know who I a-a-am' – See?"

Things were really getting out of hand. Outside the County Courthouse in Penas Grandes, a man on an accordion regularly played

Flaco Jimenez polkas, and two traffic ticket violators who came to pay about $90 each started dancing polkas on the way out, and the judge joined in, dancing with them and singing along! Even the Alma Seca Police Department put a wreath of chiles on the door, and added tiny white Christmas lights to the back windows of both of its police cars. In the middle of July!

But what really irritated the Chamber of Commerce was that nobody was selling anything! Some of the local vendors ran off t-shirts marked "I Saw the Holy Tortilla" but no one bothered to buy them. People just getting there wanted to get in and see it first before it disappeared, and after people saw it, they didn't care as much about those t-shirts as about whatever shirts they already had on. People all over South Texas quit watching TV. National advertisers were angry because sales were down, and local politicians were even angrier because the election was right around the corner, but nobody showed at the free-beer political *pachangas*. They were all watching the tortilla.

The family's landlord, smart businessman that he was, tried to sell front-row seats and even tried to broker a deal with the nearest TV station to get coverage on Channel 13, but somehow the steady stream of people flowing slowly past the tortilla kept him from even getting a foothold. And when people "left".... instead of leaving, they just sat outside a while and thought, then got in line again to see what the Virgin was doing next. The big TV station from Weslaco did send several crews out, but somehow they always came back empty-handed. There was nothing on the tape. Maybe the equipment had malfunctioned or maybe they'd forgotten to turn the cameras on. No one knew, because the tape had been sent back with someone else. The cameramen had stayed behind, to hang out some more with the tortilla.

An anonymous complaint was brought before the county judge, but the judge, who was speaking a lot of Spanish these days, just smiled and said he saw no reason *"pa' quejarse tanto.* Just relax, *ese!* Things'll work out."* The deputy tried to get him to re-consider, but it was close to 5 p.m. and the judge said he had to leave, because a *primo* was coming over and they were gonna go watch the tortilla.

Word of the holy tortilla kept spreading. People from all parts of the world arrived daily, flying into San Antonio and driving south in rented cars, or hitching rides with religious caravans of old minivans, low-riders, and rusted-out gas-guzzlers coming from San Antonio's

West Side, Austin's East Side, and Falfurrias' downtown! They arrived at all hours of the day and night, pouring in with little concern for hotel or food, but all eager to see what the Virgin was doing now. Everyone seemed to interpret her actions in their own way. A major French theologian came to write her post-doctoral dissertation on it. Some said her decision to write it began the day The Virgin Above The Tortilla had sat facing the opposite direction, shoulders curled forward, and a small child had said loudly, "Maybe she's reading to her kids!" Maria del Rosario said this same moment was what decided her to become a Literacy Teacher.

⸻◆⸻

     The Council of Bishops was, frankly, pissed. None of the regional reports had been sent in, nothing came into the Archbishop's Special Collections, and the local priest never returned their calls. In addition, they had received numerous complaints, in confidence, from the Archbishop in Mexico City in whose archdiocese the ORIGINAL sighting of the Virgin of Guadalupe had occurred, he reminded them, some 460 years before. The Bishops were in the process of calling in a team of experts to challenge the tortilla's authenticity.

     Word was there were now numerous government agents infiltrating the crowd. The people of Alma Seca and surrounding areas weren't much upset by the ruckus, but the rest of the nation seemed to be in quite a stir. Dallas papers reported something about lack of ethnic representation for whites, males, and Protestants, and one newspaper in the Northeast even ran headlines reading "Steaming Vapors Cult in South Texas Threatens Ethnic Unrest." The scariest part about it, it seemed, was that no actual footage was available. According to the papers this was due to "a communications blockade by local terrorist groups and overall heightened security." The National Enquirer tried to run a story on it, but every time they assigned someone, that person ended up heading off for South Texas and never coming back!

     Soon bomb threats were arriving at the Courthouse, where the judge just laughed and said, "*¡Que Gacho!*"

⸻◆⸻

No one knows who really did it. Some blamed Washington, and some blamed Rome. Others said Fidel Castro had a hand in it. Chicano rights activists in California said they had proof that Skinheads and other white racist groups were involved. Memo Canales, an old *Movimiento*-activist and community organizer, told his friends he strongly suspected the Governor, who sprinkled Spanish words into his speeches generously before elections, but never did much for the Spanish-speaking other than to divide their vote.

Whoever did it, it was done. Thirty packs of plastique were tied together and thrown in a window, to land right on top of the tortilla. The tortilla was totally destroyed.

The miracle was - no one was injured, and except for a lot of dust and smoke, and a few leftover *regalos* from France and South Africa, the family's home remained much as it had been before the day the Virgin came to dance above a disc of steaming *masa*. The people of Alma Seca seemed relatively calm about the whole thing, just kind of shrugged their shoulders like at the end of a good honeymoon, and went on about their work with a little smile still on their lips. The songs were still sung, the stories still told, and people said they could still close their eyes and see her, clearly framed by the sun's rays, moving about the daily tasks that they saw reflected in their own lives. Some said that the air in Alma Seca smelled different now. Fresher, greener, kind of like corn stalks. Some said their skin did too.

The smell of corn stalk, of freshness followed the visitors as well, and they went home with a sense they had carried something new back with them, something red or a folkloric blue-green or quiet, or spangled with stars or tiny Christmas lights.

Local officials and the Chamber of Commerce breathed a sigh of relief. Washington, Mexico City, Rome, all breathed in relief as well. And the governor went back to promising he would improve education, especially for minorities, by rewarding those schools whose test scores were high, and punishing those whose scores weren't. And slowly, people began to return to their normal lives, attending the miracle room at the local church and gathering with *familia* on their front porches.

No one remembered the rest of the *masa*, still in the back of the top shelf of the woman's refrigerator. No one remembered, either, that the youngest child had eaten of it.

The Pot has Eyes

"The *jarro* has eyes, and it's looking at me."

"No, *Mamá*, you're only imagining it."

"No, go imagine yourself! This is real!"

"Mamá, it's the same bean pot we've made beans in for years!"

"No, it's not, don't you remember? That one broke. Sometime after your father died. It couldn't bring itself to make good beans again anyway!"

"*Pero, Mamá* . . ."

"No, we bought this one at the H.E.B. It was sitting there between the shiny aluminum pots and the blue *peltre* camping stuff that the gringos like to hang on their walls. And aluminum's not good for you anyway!"

"*¿Pero, que tiene eso que ver, Mamá?* That doesn't make the pot have eyes!"

"This one does."

"It's just the design on it, the way the paint circles around two little round things."

"They're not round things! They're eyes."

"So if it's got eyes, they're blind, okay?"

"Not this one, it sees. Not only that, it's criticizing!"

"What is it criticizing, *Mamá?* The two of us and our raggedy clothes and funny lives? None of my clothes fit anymore, they all have holes, we don't have money to go buy all that expensive stuff they're selling, and you're worried about an old bean *jarro!*" – whined the daughter, trying to adjust the off-center skirt of her dress.

"*Tú anda*, ignore me if you want, but you know I'm telling the truth. The *jarro* has eyes!"

"Ok, so if the *jarro* has eyes, what can we do about it anyway? If it'll make you happy, I'll throw it in the trash. Nobody has time to make beans anymore anyway. We get 'em out of a can and warm 'em in the microwave. So I'll throw it out, just quit talking *locuras*, Mom, it makes me nervous!"

"No!!!" the old lady screamed, "Don't throw it away!!! Then you'll *never* get rid of it. It wants us to see something."

"Should I ask? Maybe I don't want to ask this question, *Mamá*, maybe I'm tired of this, and I just want to close my eyes and not hear you worry it anymore. Life is just a headache, and keeping my eyes open to hear *ideas locas* just makes it hurt worse!"

The old lady turned to face the pot, and began her appeal in a low rumble, as the sour-faced daughter leaned back on the sofa, defeated, and rolled her eyes to the ceiling.

"I don't know what you want, pot, but you have to quit watching us - you have to let us know what you want and then just go your way. *Déjanos, por favor.*" The last three words were half prayer, half scolding, but the clay pot didn't leave them alone. It just kept its eyes open and watched as the old lady tossed and turned in the afternoon heat of her aching bed.

By nightfall, the old lady had risen to rummage through the refrigerator. Age and exhaustion had robbed the leftovers in the small bowls of any attempt at flavor, and she found nothing that would satisfy. She considered approaching the bean pot and cooking something special from scratch, but she was still too annoyed and worried to get near it. She covered it gently with a dishcloth, clean but worn thin at the edges. A moment later, she removed the dishcloth, afraid it would offend the pot's very open eyes. She stared at it. Asked of it, "What do I do?" She paced. Then, finally, she put on the faded black sweater, more from custom than from chill, and went out the door to she knew not where.

Walking down the broken sidewalk of the *barrio* streets, she passed a girl with purple hair and an earring through her tongue. The girl's thick, black eye makeup made her eyes look all-consuming, sad and piercing, as if they could swallow up all the tragedies of the world. Three boys hung out at a corner, outside the small grocery store, their hair cut in odd shapes and angles. The old lady was frightened by their hairstyles, jolted by the look so unnatural to the way they had looked as children. One had his hair long on the top half of his head and shaved bald on the bottom half. Four earrings stood out on each of his two ears, and one on his lip. The second one's hair was bleached an extreme blonde, a color that, next to his dark skin, blinded her. His eyes seemed a pale fish-blue, not like human eyes at all, but reflective like the scales of a fish, and clouded like the cataracts of the aged. For a moment, the hair of the third seemed to make sense, something she recognized in this strange new world. It was the proud Indian cut of the Mohawk. Frightening, but still recognizable. Something she could find some root, some history for. So shook she was by the styles of the young men around her, that she took some comfort in his standing-up-straight strip of hair from his forehead to his *nuca*, not caring to notice or being able to absorb the reality of its pink and blue rainbow coloration.

Inside the store, she could smell the temptation of the burritos, tacos and corn dogs sitting under the hot lamp, but so accustomed was she to not buying the ready-made or individually served that she passed by without even considering it and headed to the few shelves of cans and packages. She picked out a package of *Masa Harina* for corn tortillas, and then moved to the bin of lonely and bruised vegetables, where she uncharacteristically selected an avocado without checking its price. Riding high on some intoxication of mission, she added a tomato, a lemon, another avocado and two *serrano chiles*.

At the checkstand, she hesitated a second at her extravagance, suddenly lost.

"Did you change your mind?" scowled the tired, middle-aged woman who even ten years ago would have added "*Señora*" and a smile to that same question.

The old woman woke from her hesitation and emptied the last few dollars and the food stamp card from her sweater pocket. As she exited the store, holding the small plastic bag, she paused to tell the third of the young boys, "I like your hair" at which the young man was caught off guard, and the other two hooted and burst into laughter. The pink and blue changed slightly in shade as his complexion deepened. The old woman, frightened by the looks of the other two still, and by their loud behavior, wavered in balance as she hurried down the block.

The old woman passed a young mother stuffed tightly into a tank top and short, black skirt, with a crying toddler running after her. The child was dressed only in diapers and a dirty shirt.

"I'm NOT going to carry you, you fatso! An' you better hurry up or I'll just leave you at home alone, *chiflado!*"

The child cried even harder, and the young woman looked even more irritated, more angry, part of her wishing that someone could carry *her*, and dry *her* tears. She needed to use the restroom, but the gas station across the street had now locked its restrooms to everyone except the employees. A well-dressed man in a shiny new car drove slowly past, giving her the eye, and she walked even faster so the toddler would not be part of the picture he saw. He looked away. She knew that in twenty minutes he could be across town, in a neighborhood where the streets had no chug holes and the gas stations all left their restrooms open, where the clerks at the store always smiled and asked if they could help you find anything else, and where their eyes did not follow you inside the store to see if you were stealing something. Angry, she picked up her pace, and the child's tears ran even faster down his shirt to further soak the wet and shredding diaper.

The old woman, too, had seen the well-dressed man. She did not trust him, did not trust much of what she saw around her. Others dressed like him had come to her door, always making promises, always asking for a signature, always stealing what was not theirs.

The path back to her house suddenly seemed longer, more frightening, and the steps seemed more difficult. She no longer recognized the streets, and without warning, her head suddenly felt without strength, without light, without direction

———•+•———

The first thing she saw when she opened her eyes was the bean pot. Its eyes were worried, its hair was pink and blue and cut in the style of the Mohawk Indian, and it talked.

"Are you okay?" the bean pot asked.

She jolted upright. It was not a bean pot after all. It was the young man with the standing-straight-up Indian hair.

"Are you okay?" he repeated. "I didn't know what to do, but I see you leave this house usually, so when you fainted, I brought you back here. Is that okay? Are you alright?"

It took the old woman a minute to make sense of the sequence of events. Her daughter was not there, had probably gone searching for her. The young man seemed embarrassed, tried to explain. "I'm the one from the store, remember? You said you liked my hair."

"You look like an *indio*."

The young man didn't know if it was a compliment or a cut-down till the old lady's dark coffee eyes crinkled, remembering, and she whispered "*Mi papá era indio. Apache.*"

Then, hesitantly, she asked, "You did not come to rob me? Why did you do this?"

The young man did not know what to answer. Finally he responded quietly, "I like your hair?" And neither could explain why, but that made them both laugh harder than either had done in quite a while.

⋅—◆—⋅

By the time the daughter rejoined them, the old lady had made and salted a whole plate of avocado tacos, and the young man was eating enthusiastically, the wild Mohawk he had so carefully admired in his broken mirror this morning now dipping in time to his bites from the tacos. The corn tortillas were soft and handmade, and the flavors of the tomato, lemon and serrano had already kissed the avocado. The beans were just starting to boil, but the smell was warm and pleasing.

"You look kind of like my grandmother. I used to have a grandmother when I was little," he mumbled confidently, between bites. The young man could hardly believe the strangely delicious and comforting taste of these incredible homemade tacos. Maybe she would make them again. Maybe she would teach him how to make those beans. Maybe she would like the new shade he was thinking of dying his hair.

His smile was interrupted for just a moment by a look of disbelief, as he thought he saw the pot, from its comfortable perch on the stove, smiling back at him.

THE MOUNTAINS,
the TREES, the RIVER
this DIRT . . .
the WHOLE FAMILIA

Inheritance

"I own this place!"

I whipped my head up to see an old woman coming at me, limping through the summer-high weeds on an arthritic leg. Her shout startled me, for I had jumped the fence to get in, and climbed over the gate with that new brass lock.

"I own this place!! I own more, too. Down alla way to the river from here! You can still smell it, can't you?"

Her accusation was right. There was a coolness in my nostrils that smelled like the thirsty little river I had just walked beside minutes before. The dirt had crumbled softly off the edge from under the roughly velveted buffalo grass, and my foot had slipped into the dark river water. The river flowed past, seeming to carry the centuries with it as well, but I had been unable to force out the smell of wet, pungent dirt, of musky river in my nose, a smell that still followed me like an intoxication.

There was more. More that my guilt at trespassing made me fear she would know as well. The river had reached out for me. The cool, protective shade of the pecan trees and the sweet pervasive smell of the musky water had calmed the hot, bright headache of the brush country above. The tiny delicate fingers of mesquite leaves had whispered rhythmically with each wave of wind. My lungs had inhaled the quiet, and it had adopted me. It had taken me a long while to convince myself, almost regretfully, to climb back up the slope toward the road, as the trees grew sparse again, my legs grew tired, and the weeds grew thicker and dryer. Then, I had been possessed by the strange impulse to jump the ugly metal gate on this small *acrecito*, this tiny acre whose other three sides were bordered by a homemade barbed wire fence of crooked posts that had once been tree limbs.

But her voice had shaken me deeply, into something beyond guilt and fear, into a stunned and echoing silence.

". . . It has something in it. The dirt slips off the edge and into the water . . . *así suavecito*, so quiet. Then it gets washed up again, to the sides, *¡y a'i vamos otra vez! Pos,* this many acres away, we still smell it. In the nose."

"It stays with you, *ya ves?* It doesn't go away. My great–gramma knew that. I still hear her sometimes."

She was staring at the dirt on her *chanclas*, and her eyes were wet with love. She trembled out a sigh so long and shaky I was afraid she would collapse. But she didn't. She kept talking, her words colored by passion, her stories flowing like the currents, one into the next.

"*A-a-a-ay,* my great–gramma! She was always on this river! The day she was born she went into it. All newborn and sticky in the heat of summer, they dipped her in. Pos y from then on, she was always stuck to this river. She used to play there while her father worked.

"He used to make big wooden ladles, *a mano,* from the branches that dropped there, right on the banks, *pero* way up the river, where downtown is now. He said the water made the wood more *suavecita* – *la curaba!* And where they put that tortilla warmer on a broomstick – *¿como le pusieron?* – Oh, *sí,* The Tower of the Americas! *Pos,* that's where her mother would pluck chickens! A little further down the river, where all those expensive restaurants are now, that's where she'd play or just sit alone, hearing the trees sing and feeling the wet earth of its edges on her toes. . . .

"And when she was a girl, *venía un indio.* This Indian hid behind the bushes and threw pebbles at her until she'd see him and run, screaming *¡Ay vienen los indios! ¡Ay vienen los indios!* (The Indians are com–mi–i–ing!) Then he'd laugh so hard and she'd hear him! *¡Y se enojaba!* She'd get mad all the time. Till finally one day she stayed, and got mad, and threw pebbles right back at him!

"They got married later, *y allí mero pusieron su casa.* That's where they built that little house where all ten of the kids were born. And one was my gramma, the one who died so young, right by the river, near *el Alamo,* while her young daughter played.

"And my gramma used to wash clothes in the San Antonio River, all'a time, close to where they put that new hotel – *¿como se llama?* – Hell–tone, *o algo.* They put it up all in a week, *¿no te acuerdas? Ya 'staba* built! They just brought in the rooms and stacked them up, like blocks – like *juguetitos.* They still look like little toys.

"You can hardly see the sun from there anymore – her clothes would have never dried on the rocks *con esa sombra grandota!* No matter. Those fancy tourists walk there now, but they put their pretty perfumes on, and walk where my gramma washed out the sweat and the dirt from her clothes!! The sad thing is . . . they don't even smell it.

"But the part near the river we hadn't used yet – we started at this end. River front property *que quién sabe qué.* They took that too."

The old woman was quiet for too long. For some reason, the ache inside me sharpened.

"I been here too long, *ves?*" she said gently, as she picked up a dry cracked cake of the dark brown dirt, smiling, turning it slowly in her palm like a large medallion, "Its color is my color."

The softness was gone, the spirit back, in her sharp whisper: "I own it."

She sat back on a smooth stone and pointed in the direction of a small mesquite tree near the gate. The small brass lock flashed in the sunlight but seemed not to glisten as much as the medallion of dirt in her hands.

"Over there, by *el mesquite,* that's just the part we started with, maybe, oh, thirty or forty bodies ago."

"*¿Tan pocos?*"

"*Pos,* I forget how many. I think more."

An uncomfortable swelling began to bother my chest. I tried to keep my mind here, now, on this strange old lady, but a shallower voice kept washing in on the edges, slipping off pieces of my concentration. The conversation I'd had with my cousin a few weeks before haunted me, left me with a dry, unsettled feeling in my throat:

> "Well, I'd like to leave it open, Mary Beatriz, but we just can't take that chance anymore. I mean, last month, there was an unauthorized burial there. That person may not have even belonged to our church!"
>
> My cousin pronounced this last word the same way she would have announced an alien from a UFO, or worse, a Communist. So the lock had been left on the front gate, and my cousin's answer had been left on the doorstep of my yet–open mouth: "We have no idea what KIND of a body is there!"
>
> As she talked, my mind flooded with images of my great-grandfather, the preacher, haggling eighty years ago with the preacher of the Baptist church, till he got the four dollar deal on the four acres and the deed given in his name. Three of the acres were the driest and the most treeless, but the fourth reached down to the river. The Baptist preacher had finally

given in on the request because of one last afterthought: "If we don't say yes, he'll probably come to me next time one of his poor Mexican Greasers dies, and ask for me to let them in OUR graveyard. And the sisters in the front row will never stop fussing to me if they think we let just ANY kind of body in our little plot."

So, reluctantly, he had signed the paper, and cut his nice six-teen acre property into a twelve acre property (the number the Lord had chosen for his disciples.) There would still be more than enough room for many shady burials under the oaks, for peaceful baptisms without competing congregations and for enough acreage to hunt deer and rabbits for parishioners in need. He had asked just one favor in return: that they begin their burials at the far end, up by the road, so as to allow his church some "adjustment time" for the proximity.

"Well, does it matter what kind of a body is there?" I'd foolishly asked. "I mean, obviously, it's a dead body. Isn't there plenty of room?"

"Well, this property belongs to our congregation, and the church board has to make all the decisions on who's allowed."

The old woman sighed, and it pulled me back.

"So they sent us down the river, and then off the river. To here – so far down – and off – that it's almost not San Antonio – almost not anywhere. All'a'way back into this *rinconcito* so hidden they still don't know it's here, almost. Maybe that's a good thing...

"And I own this. I bought it. With my family. With that stone there, and that one. And with the one for the three babies, *pobrecitos*. And with my tears that have made it rich. . . .

"You don't see much here, jus' a few weeds and a little tiny shade, but there's a lot here anyway. From the other *siglos*, you know, too. Especially down in the riverbed – maybe still a ladle or two my *tata-ra–abuelo* threw away – and some arrowheads (or maybe jus pebbles) from my *viz–abuelo*. An' the stuff that goes in that don't show – the blood an' the afterbirth, the sweat, the *lágrimas* – the stuff that gives power.

"*Sí*. I'm from San Antonio," she said proudly, and then began to chuckle. "Or maybe, San Antonio, it's from me."

"Like these little babies here —" she said, touching the narrow stone lovingly, as if it were a child's hair she was stroking out of its forehead.

"From me, but from some place else. I can see 'em here, hear 'em. Not everyplace this strong – you don't get good – uh, *como* TV? – *Eso*, reception!

"But here, *sí*. I hear'em all here, even my mother. Even my great–gramma, and her *indio querido*, and maybe even his grandparents.

"I hear 'em singing, talking, even this many acres away from the river – this far down from the rest of what I own.

"I know they got rich people with papers, with houses, with deeds, oth–orrity! Thass o.k. – it goes in too – the papers, the houses – it goes into the same dirt . . . after 'while. 'Cause they owe me rent. I own this place."

Her eyes were wet and her voice matter-of-fact as she said quietly, "Nobody gone take it away. It's mine. It's ours, *m'ija*."

As she spoke the word *m'ija*, the word I had heard so often as a child, the warmth of her dark brown cheekbones, the curve of her nose suddenly focused my eyes. A warm flow of strength seemed to be surging from inside my veins, through the curve of my nose, the color of my cheekbones.

"Don't you remember how I always tol' you that, when you were *chiquititita, así*, and I'd rock you in my arms, *así*, and I'd show you everything that was yours. *Así*.

"Your eyes are wet, *m'ija*. *Ahora sí me reconociste*. This sun makes it hard to see sometimes. And this last month has been very *pesado* for you. But take this – all of this – it will give you *fuerza* – from everything that's in it, and everyone.

"It's ours because we're in it. With our dreams and with our deaths and with everything that grows from it. This dirt – this dirt is full of us. *¿No ves, m'ijita?* We are made of it, and it is made of us, and we – OWN it."

———————

A country car passed slowly down the forgotten road, toward the richly-fertilized dirt of the dairy that had flourished so well on these hidden outskirts of town, and the passengers wondered at the solitary figure they saw sitting on a stone in the tiny cemetery, across from a newly placed tombstone, a young woman whose wet eyes stared at something in her hand as if it had been handed to her.

"Poor thing," they said, "Out there all alone – in that little old cemetery. You spose she's got somebody buried there? With as poor as that little cemetery is, whoever it is that's there probably didn't even leave nothin' to 'er anyway."

Fourteen miles up the river, a piece of dark brown dirt slid softly off the edges of the old river's bank that graced the Hilton Palacio del Rio's stylish cafe tables and slipped into the water that headed slowly downstream to a place the city had almost forgotten.

Whispers From the Dirt

March 2, 1836: San Antonio, Tejas, República de México

The water trickled through her toes, and the wind through her hair. There was no one else to play with. Except the trees. And the Dirt maybe, but *She* was always so quiet. *She* let the others do the talking. And Tacha liked to talk.

"I'm here!!" Tacha announced. "Now what do you have for me today?" A leaf fell from the tree. *"Es todo?"* she scolded, acting a little *chiflada*, a little like her mother would never let her act at home.

A small twig fell as the wind picked up. "That's better," Tacha answered, glad to have more company. She had always hated being alone, hated having no one to play with, no one to talk to.

"Now I can make a flag," she touted, twisting the twig through one end of the yellow-green leaf, and planting the small flag in the soft wet dirt of the river's edge. "Here! I'll put up a new flag just like they did over *el Álamo*. So what shall we play?" she turned to the wind, and it blew the small flag very, very hard, but the flag did not fall apart.

"I'm here," the Dirt whispered to her, but Tacha did not hear, for she was already hard at play, building small houses out of straws.

⤙•⧟•⤚

"¿Dónde estará?" the frantic woman moaned pleadingly as she searched for her small daughter. "She was here just one minute ago!" Yanking off the nailed boards from the window, she scanned the neighbors' yards, the stillness of the street, the empty plaza, the strange new flag over the mission, her heart sinking with each empty garden. Then she saw the sliver of light that escaped the unlocked doorbolt. "The river," her heart whispered to her, and she tore out of the door, leaving everything open behind her.

March 2, 2006: San Antonio, Texas, USA

The hospital was ice cold and full of white noise that irritated the old woman. The staff was even colder.

Her eyes screamed, *"Por favor!* I'm here. I'm here. I'm not dead yet! You move me this way and that – you check my chart, my lungs, my blood pressure, you never look at my eyes. Won't anybody look at me, *por favor?* Can't you hear me? My mouth can't say the words, but I'm still here, I'm here! Look at me!! *¡No me abandonen!"*

The doctor flipped through the charts impatiently, but didn't find the necessary forms.

"Can you get me what I need on THIS one?" His voice had scraped like rough sandpaper over the nursing staff's competence. The nurse scooted quickly out of the hospital room, and headed to the floor station, but not before he saw that look on her face. He knew she hated being on duty when he was here, knew he was known for his no–nonsense attitude; anything out of line, he shot straight and sharp.

Dr. Rodriguez glanced at his watch, and felt a bad mood beginning to grip at his jaw and throb his temples. He hated incompetence, hated wasted time. He realized he'd been grinding his teeth together, and took a deep, purposeful breath. With so many good things time could be spent on. . . .

He looked out from the hospital window at a green clump of trees in the distance and remembered the sprawling, ancient trees they had strolled past on the Riverwalk at lunch. His pulse slowed at the memory. That place had always been special to them. It hadn't been hard to decide where to make their vows – that old church, the plaza nearby that dated back to before the Alamo. It didn't feel ancient. It just felt like home.

A spring-breezed lunch at the patio tables outside the Palacio del Rio had been followed by a delicious walk along the river, a walk so slow that schedules and emergencies and timelines seemed to drift far away, like tiny leaves in the river's current. Her playful smile, her sense of humor, never failed to soften the sharp set of his jaw, to slow the impatient pace of his habitual drive. They'd passed the plaque that marked the tree where snipers climbed to pick off defenders of the

Alamo, defenders who sneaked out of the besieged mission to run to the river for water.

"So I guess it was you that was the sniper and me that was the defender, huh?"

"All depends," he smiled, with a guileful arch in his eyebrows, "on what it was that was being defended . . . I was just being a good patriot, defending the Republic of Mexico, fighting for freedom and upholding the Mexican constitution's emancipation of all slaves. YOU GUYS were the Texian Rebels, defending your right to own slaves and to rebel against the government you'd promised to uphold."

"Oooh," she winced. "*Touché*. I promise to be extra careful next time I wage any rebellions against *you!*" she laughed. The gold in her hair gleamed in the tree-filtered sun. After another bend in the river, she'd asked, "So you think any of your ancestors were up there sniping?"

"Maybe," he said. "Maybe some out there defending too, getting water."

"You've always had a thing for water . . ."

"I've always had a thing for you," he admitted sheepishly, fingers lightly touching her cheek. She took his fingers to her lips and kissed them gently, "I like the color of you."

"What? Remind you of a dark California tan?"

"No, more like a San Antonio earth brown."

"The original Southwestern look," he joked, then laid his hand softly beside hers and said quietly, "Nice color combination. High contrast, but still – two earthtones, yours golden sand and mine adobe."

"Lucky for me you like that color scheme. The nurses at the hospital tell me you're pretty tough on everything you *don't* like."

He shrugged, in painful admission, as if embarrassed at his own helplessness to change. She laughed at his wincing confession and grabbed him in a tight body hug, easily loving the little boy weakness in him more than she did the sharp-shooter finesse. He tried to keep secret his relief that she, at least, would not leave him for being himself; without her, he had always felt so very alone.

———

"I'm here," said the old husband to his wife.

The old man had slipped in the door, and was talking to the still body as if she could understand him. Dr. Rodríguez raised his eyebrow. He reached into his shirt pocket for the polished dark wood pen, but found first a small yellow–green leaf. It must have fallen on him at lunch, or as they strolled under the trees. For just a moment, his fingers rubbed it, felt the infinitely fine sand on its smooth surface, the warmth of sunlight seeming to still gleam from it. He thought of her, wondered if this old man had ever thought of his wife that way.

He looked again at the bed-bound patient. At the brown face that must have once been young and full of dreams. At the frightened eyes that were open, dark, as hard to see beneath as the river water. He lifted the pen, debating. . . . The thought trickled through him as naturally as the final decision.

Perhaps we could re–evaluate the prognosis. Just in case. She is, after all, still alive, and where there's life, there's hope, isn't there?

March 2, 1836: San Antonio, Newly Declared Republic of Texas

The adobe-skinned man sat hunched on the hardened earth, his lower back against the inside of the mission walls, his head slumped into his trembling hands. The quiet of the city bothered him, the only sounds that of the siege of soldiers outside, encamped in worried wait-ing. His ears searched for the occasional voice from the city that the wind carried up and over the walls, to where he sat, listening. That last voice – was it . . . ?

He closed his eyes and shuddered, the cool wind touching him in consolation.

"CURSED MEXICANS!"

The words jolted him. Sam was at the top of the walls, looking over.

"They got snipers up in the trees. Hope Billy makes it okay. I'm aimin' for those trees – anything moves, I'll get it."

Worry made the man on the ground try to soften the hardness of the old scout.

"Be careful, Sam, *por favor*. There's a whole town moving out there. My town."

"Don't worry, most of your kind moved their families outta the city when they knew ole Santy Ana was comin' with the whole Mexican army. Or was your family one o' those 'at stayed around to be near you, case you needed 'em? You told your wife and daughter t'stay outta the way, right?"

Sam's eye returned to the rifle sights, and the man on the ground closed his eyes in prayer.

━━⬩━━

"*Mamá!* Why are you running so fast?" Tacha shouted. She opened her mouth again to ask more, but a loud crack jolted her, and something warmer than the wind whistled past as her mother screamed. The tree beside Tacha took the first bullet, but the woman running at full pace to reach her child took the second.

Tacha felt the heat so near it stunned her, and something seemed very wrong with her mother. Tacha was shaking with fear as she pulled on her mother's shoulder insistently, but *Mamá* didn't answer.

"*Mamá, Mamá!* What's wrong! Something's wrong!"

More bullets cracked the air beside her, and Tacha, clinging still to the shoulder of *Mama's* splattered dress, jumped as a man fell out of the trees. His brown face lay still and bleeding on the dirt a few feet away. Another crack and she heard a body's odd splash, as a man with blond hair fell into the river, still hugging a large water jug. Then, it was quiet, and the bullets stopped. So quiet, the life and light seemed to drain from the sun.

Mamá was still and full of blood. Tacha's breaths were coming in quick gasps between the sobs, and she whimpered, "I don't want – to be alone. . . . Please, *Mamá* – don't leave me – alone. I'm scared. I'm sca-ared. I don't want – to be – a-lo-o-one."

This time, *She* answered back clearly and without hesitation.

"Don't worry," said the Dirt, gently, "I'm here. I'll always be here."

Reclaiming

This is told in retrospect, looking back on my life from the unique vantage point of not having yet been born. I can remember everything perfectly, all the way up to the hour of my death. That's because our memory is perfect and complete when first given the piece of dirt and water to make us. The rocks and sun come later. Last is wind, but by that time, it's too late. We've forgotten our life, cause we're too busy living it. We've forgotten lots of things. Like how the pieces of us are all around. And how pieces of everything all around are inside of us.

But for now, it's all here. I can hear it, like voices. I hear the traffic right behind you this moment, up on the street, and the traffic the way it was on my first day of school. And how it was when I lay in the hospital dying, looking so old and fragile they didn't even talk to me the way you talk to an adult anymore.

I even remember the way the traffic was before the me that is Me was me.

– There goes a deer!

– You get it, with your arrow. I'll scare it towards you.

– Naaah, too late.

– You shouldda gone for it, Huilta. We'll probably go days without another good chance like that!

– Hey, this place is nice. The water, the trees. I feel good here.

– Huilta, we gotta keep moving if we're gonna get any food.

– I like it here. . . . There's mesquite beans over there. And look, Yantli – berries!

– It is cool under these trees, but . . .

– Maybe we could call it Yanaguana, place of the quiet water. Maybe we should stay . . .

<hr />

– Enrique, aquí! Let's set up camp here! The place where the river winds up close to the trees.

– Hey, it's not a bad place to camp while we look for a good fort site.

– Yeah, I'm tired. Did you just see a rabbit go by? Who knows? Maybe we won't need to go look for a good fort site. Maybe we'll stay here.

<hr />

– Moisés, maybe this would be a good place to stay... far from the offices of the *Propaganda Fide*. . . .

<hr />

– Billie, isn't this a nice place? Seems friendlier than where we been before. I'd love to stay someplace friendly for a change, someplace quiet. . . .

<hr />

– Ilse, maybe we'll stay . . .

<hr />

– Mui, why don't we stay here? We could open a Vietnamese Restaurant and send Mama money. . . .

<hr />

It all goes back. But if you won't look back, you'll never see forward. I can tell you that cause here I am at the beginning, which makes me see my end too. It all goes round, like in a circle. We end up where we started, only smoother, like a wheel that's gone round a few times.

Well, don't worry about it too much if it bothers you, just let me go ahead and tell you what I remember. Right from here, inside this womb. Where I can see things better, just being straight what they are, without interference.

I was about nine years old, I guess, and I fell into the river. That's right. Kind of baptized myself in the San Antonio River, by accident. I was reaching for minnows, and leaned over too far. Or maybe it called me. Or maybe, something inside me was calling it.

The dirt stayed in my shoes. The clothes got all washed out and everything, but the dirt never quite left my shoes. Got ground up real fine, and worked in through my skin. We are what we eat, you've heard 'em say it. We are what we step on, too.

A handful or two of years after that, we were driving, my family and I, on Highway 10, someplace on the way to California, someplace maybe in New Mexico. We were headed to see my cousins. We were just out someplace in the middle of nowhere driving, when we passed, in the middle of flat nothing, this mountain range way off to my right. Thank God I wasn't driving the car cause I'd a never heard the end of it. I would've pulled straight off the road and gone wagoning over the desert to those mountains. They were calling me so clear it wouldda taken a mean old man with a hole in his chest 'stead of a conscience to ignore it. I just wanted to go, to head straight over without a thought, to reach for those mountains as automatically as your lungs grab for air. My heart went off, bumping over the rocks and the nothingness towards the mountain, but the car kept going the direction it had been and no one else knew anything'd happened.

But something in me stayed lost out in that desert, wanting to go off to the mountains, and find what it was that was missing from me over there. Took me years to figure it out. But now I know.

Ever wonder what happens to all that dirt that people wash off of their clothes, tears that wash out of their eyes, dirt that falls off of their shoebottoms and into the river, earth that floats away? Ever wonder where all that dust goes that blows around and you have to shake off of you on windy days?

It knows what it does. It goes where it wants to go. It piles itself up to split that river two ways. Or stop it altogether. It shifts itself over to make a refreshing little pool of comfort, or spreads itself out to get a garden going. Or piles itself up high to create its own monument, to shape its own mountain.

The way I figure it, there were pieces of me up there in those mountains. Minerals from my tears, silt from my riverbedded shoes or from my dreams of things I'd wanted to do or reach for, dirt from old sloughed–off skin cells, stuff from hurts I'd dusted off a long while ago. There were brothers of my bones up there, and sisters of my skin. Those rocks were cousins, the weeds growing up between them my own stubborn memories. I was headed off to the right for a family reunion. It was made of me. And I was made of it.

I'd seen that place lots of times before, every summer that we'd headed to California, but this was just the first time they'd talked to me. First time I heard their voices.

I remember other voices too. There were voices that night we danced in the old courtyard that used to be General Cos' patio, in *La Villita*, "The Town", the old part of San Antonio. It was wonderful to dance in celebration of our wedding in this place where even a hundred years before, others celebrated their weddings.

Your black curls tossed by the breeze and the music, your eyes dancing reflections of the river water, the color of your hands singing earthcolors – we swirled to the music of polkas and waltzes. It was a wonderful wedding!

But we didn't dance at my wedding. At least not in the photos. Not at the reception. Not on the plaza. The fundamentalist side of the family would have been offended, so there was no dance, just mariachis that we all listened to, tapping our feet. . . .

It was the wedding party of 100 years ago – or no, 150 years ago. But I remember it. I heard the voices of the guests. And ours. I heard the music. Perhaps it was my bones, reborn of theirs, that remembered. But whatever, whenever, we were there together.

I remember another time, a time that kind of freezes inside and never goes away, even with all the other times happening at the same time. It was a tiny white box, small enough for my dark, lean, six–foot–four Texan Indian of a baby brother to carry in his arms as if he were cradling it. He knelt and laid it down in the hole that was way too big, as if the people digging it had forgotten and thought it was for a regular size coffin.

It was five-ish, with the sun not set but lowered, a week almost to the hour, after she'd been born. The cut up my belly still burned, and I couldn't reach down to touch the dirt, but your cut inside was burning so much you couldn't do anything but touch that dirt. You handed me a clump of it, and took one for yourself, and we, who had first dreamed of her, and felt her, and heard her, and loved her, and given her up to the earth, were the first to let that dirt sift through our fingers, and back onto that tiny wooden box that held her smile and her yawn and her fingers and her flesh.

Another time, I was donating blood. It's always hurt. I get kinda spots before my eyes, and have to sit down again. Something to do with not enough bodyweight. But it goes back in and keeps the flow going someplace else, in some other body. When Hemisfair opened in San Antonio back in 1968, the whole rest of the world got a chance to fall in love with the city that we could proudly beam at like glowing parents and say, "We've always loved Her." But they had to re–channel and confine and create and concrete bank and pump in and pump out and do things to – that this poor river had NEVER thought anyone could do to a river. It worried me a little, all those tubes connected to her, like IV's. But She came through it fine, and we still know, still feel her pumping through us like veins, the life–giving stream of this place, of these people. The operation came out okay because the flow reconnects us, lets those touch who need to touch – let's us all remember.

She does this, and She reclaims us. We just let Her blood pump through us, and we reclaim our past. Draw on it, like drinking moisture and minerals in through the roots, and add it to our growth, and make it a part of our present.

She's ours anyway, you know. We, who sweat and drive through traffic and pay our rent and wash our dirty towels and work sixty hours a week. We who cry our tears here and fight our fights and dance on Saturday night and sweat tons and drink tons, we have a joint title. To this river. To this land. And the river and the land – have a joint title to us.

I remember, back in about 1934, almost twenty years before I was born, the long–leaf yellow pine of Texas became extinct. Millions of acres had been decimated, pulled up, cut down for docks, railroad cars, houses, everything. Till it was all gone.

I remember 1994, people getting surprised, to tear down an old house and pull apart boards and find a hand–painted sign "Saul Lumber Company" on this board they were gonna pay somebody to haul away. They don't understand how somebody could be so proud of the work they did on this one board of common–as–corn, long–leaf yellow pine that they would handpaint a sign on a part that wasn't even gonna show. But things come back around, one way or another, nothing gets lost. So now, people are thinking it's kind of special and they're coming back with their old boards or other old boards they found or someone else's boards they had to buy from'm and asking "Can you make a piece of furniture out of this?" or "Make me a chair that shows this name" or even "Make me a coffin of this, cause I understand old, long–leaf, yellow pine, cause now I'm extinct too."

But I remember sometime, way after I died, when one of those chairs got left out in the rain, or one of those good ole pine coffins did what good ole pine coffins are s'posed to do, and somehow or other, the dirt had its way, and some old seed trapped in a limb that got trapped in a board comes right back into its soil, and sprouts, and the whole thing starts up again.

One more thing. (Which is always a thousand more things once they start growing. But they all come back to one simple thing usually, and it's usually the dirt.) I remember me, old and ailing and everyone thinking that this time I'm not gonna make it, and I'm being real ornery and insistent that someone take down my instructions.

"Into the dirt. I want to go into the dirt. None of this mausoleum museum stuff. No crypts. Just bury me right there where my grand-parents are and my parents are and my first baby is and right next to my *querido*. And no expensive coffin. Plain pine, so it melts back easier. What kind of a field grows out of metal coffins anyway?! Or use any other kind of wood, but something easy, and nearby, like those old fenceposts over there are made of. Who cares what it looks like.

It'll look a whole lot better than I will by that point! Don't keep me well-preserved, like an expensive bottle of pickles. Just ease me right back in. I know my way around here. It's home."

"*Bueno, no le hace*, go ahead and do whatever you want. It all comes around anyway. I'm here. We're all here inside you. Talking. All at the same time. Yeah, throw the family tree in with me too, if it makes you happy. Wasn't for that much that it served anything. We're all related anyway. The whole family. You, me, everyone, the mountains, the trees, the river, and this dirt.

CHILDREN OF
CORN

El Mojado No existe

1928, Stafford, Texas

Diamante crumpled up the piece of paper and propped it between the logs. She had found it blowing in the wind in front of the sheriff's office and had saved it to help start the fire this evening. There. It would soon be hot enough to cook the soup. She stared out at the sun and decided it would not be long before her younger brothers and sister would come in from their play, asking for food and asking when Papá would be home. She hurried her steps, her ten-year-old eyes keeping watch over the sun. As she was almost done, there was a knock on the door. Her face brightened when she saw José Silva.

"*Buenas tardes.*" His dark eyes sparkled with playfulness, but his demeanor was always respectful and quiet.

"*Buenas tardes,* José. My father is not here yet, but he would love for you to join us for supper."

"*No, gracias, señorita.* I must return to the ranch to finish some chores."

(*Esos* Steubens *agarrados,* she thought, they barely give him a few hours a week to leave the ranch.)

The young *mojado* from the Steuben ranch pulled a small doll made of straw from behind his back. "And this is for you, young lady."

She started to gasp in surprise, but caught herself and said politely, "*Muchísimas gracias.* Won't you come inside?"

José walked over to the fire and sat on the small stool nearby. Diamante always tried to impress José – he was so kind and so *simpático.* Sometimes, she wondered how he could be so brave – all alone, a *mojado,* far from his family. She had her family right here all the time – her father and three younger siblings her parents had given her before Mamá passed away. She was silent for a moment – missing that strong, gentle woman who used to comb her hair into neat braids and make her soft dolls out of handkerchiefs. José saw the young girl fingering the straw doll sadly, her fingernails combing the straws on its rough yellow head. He wiped the tear off her cinnamon-milk cheek, and she quickly remembered his presence and pulled to her full height, saying, "Your gift was very kind. I'm certain the children will enjoy it, too." He started to tousle her hair, but the child had pulled on her strength and her maturity, and he did not wish to ruin her show, so he simply tipped his hat and said, "*Señorita*, I will check to see if your father is coming down the road yet."

By the time José Silva and Daniel Ibarra had reached the door, Diamante had served plates on the table for her father and his hesitant young guest. She listened with great interest to their talk, her little girl crush on the young man shining through her eyes.

"I still say they hardly pay you enough for a week's work, much less a month's. And I've seen the way they treat you."

José tried to soften the subject and convince his friend that he was satisfied. "I get my room and board and a few dollars to send to *México*. That's all I need."

"I would leave there if I were you. Neither one of those two is worth the ground they stand on."

———◆———

The paper tacked over the door said "STEUBEN RANCH." The eldest, Willie, was proud of that sign. It wore out every two months or so, but he would carefully stencil one out again, using the charcoal from the fireplace to fill in the spaces inside the block letters. It wasn't a large ranch, but it was all their German immigrant father had left them when the old man lay gasping on the metal bed and said, "*Dieses land ist jetzt Euerland*," and pointed out each of his inheritors in turn. So Willie and Max had continued plowing the fields, and Ilse would store as much of the harvest as she could in the cellar. Having the *mojado* helped. They had let him stay in the small shack behind the barn, and Ilse would take his plate to the front porch or, if he happened to be in the barn, carry it out there. In the heat of the day, as she peeled and husked and cut and salted, and as the men worked the fields, she had sometimes caught glimpses of the tall brown body, with muscles that were lean and a chest that was smooth and hairless, unlike her older brothers', whose curly hair sprouted wildly from their arms and chests. But the glimpses were few, and work was the center of each of their days.

Still, summer ripened into fall, their interactions grew longer, and one day, when she'd gone with her brothers into town, she returned to find that the day's corn harvest had already been husked and restacked into the bushel baskets, and that one tray of the tomatoes looked suspiciously clean and moist. She glanced at the darkness of the shack and whispered something under her breath that not even she herself heard.

***

"I do not like it, José," said Daniel Ibarra, his hazel eyes shooting implications beyond his words. "Pedro's parents moved to México from here before the revolution, to help her sister. Now, the grey-haired *viejitos* try to come back, so that their son can take care of them, and some uniformed *oficiante* at the border tells them that they need papers. It's ridiculous! No one asked them for papers when they left here!"

José was silent, as he usually was when his knowledgeable friend shared news and *chisme*. Daniel remembered his young friend's short amount of leisure and asked, "Was there something you wanted me to send this time?"

"Yes, if it is convenient to you."

"Of course, of course."

"Four dollars this time. Elsa talked them into raising my pay. She said they would lose me to other ranchers."

Daniel raised his eyebrows, but decided not to intrude on his friend's look of pride and pleasure, and simply accepted the worn bills, saying, "To your parents? *¿Como siempre?*" José nodded. Daniel noticed that the young man had begun to carry his shoulders straighter, and that his expressions were often filled with a vibrant color.

***

Ilse dished the food generously onto a plate and gathered a spoon, the kitchen cloth, and her cloak before she headed out. She was small and thinner than she would have liked to be. Her father had always said it was a sign of a hard worker, and of purer blood, but still – she put on her cloak to cover the outline of her collarbones before going out to take José his food. He stood when she entered the barn, and removed his hat.

"I hope it's still warm." He answered in his faltering English that the food was always good, and that she was very kind. She noticed as he smiled that the man had one tooth that gaped a bit to the side, and noted to herself that it was something like an extra smile behind his smile. That smile struck her as strangely attractive, and the peekaboo opening in it seemed to carry surprise and laughter.

She lingered. The sheriff was selling her brothers a horse, and it would take a while to work out a compromise. "That's a beautiful horse they're trying to buy. Have you seen it?"

He nodded, "I hold it for sheriff when he bring – yesterday."

"Even its hair shines," she said, trying to make use of any conversation possible.

"But not as much as yours," he thought, as he drank in her wheat-colored hair and her tightly drawn features. Somehow she heard his thought, and lowered her head, with a flush that added a special glow to her face. He lowered his head too, wanting to see more of this sunrise color to her face but scared that he might have transgressed to impropriety in his stare.

"José." The way she said it caught him off guard, as if it were the Spanish phrase "Yo sé" – I know – but stopping just short of "Yoséf." He realized it was his name and not the phrase, and liked the way the German "Y" lent a softness to the name. She must have realized how tender her voice sounded and, embarrassed, shifted to a pretense of efficient matronliness, asking if the shack was comfortable, and if there was anything he might need. "We have an extra blanket we never use – might it be of use to you?" His eyes softened in gratitude and searched hers again, as if for a moment he heard her thoughts. The laughter of the Steuben brothers and the slapping sound of pats on the back cut the air. "I'd better go now," she said, and left with just one look back, before exiting the barn door.

The next morning, she heard a soft knock on the door. José stood there, plate and spoon in hand, clean, and on top of them, the kitchen cloth she had brought him, also washed and pressed by his hands into a neatly folded square. No words passed, but he saw the sunrise growing on her cheeks again and turned quickly away, before her brothers could scold her for dallying.

As the weeks passed, his portions of food grew larger, the reasons she needed her brothers to go into town became more numerous, and José's English rapidly improved, though his moments of silence grew longer. She would sometimes glance guiltily over her shoulder, even when she knew her brothers were not on the ranch. But her heart always comforted her, reminding her that no indecency had ever been committed. After all, their time together included stares and words and smiles, but never had he so much as touched her hand. Still, she liked the way he pronounced her name "Elsa," and noticed how the soft Spanish "s" gave a special beauty to her name.

One day, during another lingering trip to the barn to take him his supper, she forgot herself while he talked of the color of the ripened squash in their fields and the leaves that were already beginning to drop from the harvest-time plants, and allowed her eyes to rest on him undisturbed – watching the smooth outline of his dark body against the sun-bleached hay, and the dance of his black eyes in front of the kerosene lamp. Suddenly, he saw her thoughts again, but even knowing this, she forgot to lower her eyes. His words had finished and he, too, simply absorbed her, and it did not occur to him to lower his eyes. The moment stood free of time and free of everything except the absorption of this somehow peaceful joy.

"Ilse! Our glasses are empty! Hurry it up, will ya?!" Max's voice jarred them, and she left without glancing back. He went quickly to his shack, this time forgetting the plate of food behind him in the barn.

The next moment they had alone together, his jaw was set and sober, "I need . . . to say." She held her breath. Both of them knew some of what he was going to say, but neither knew how much, nor what she would reply. By the time Ilse left the barn she was dazed, but she somehow felt taller and more regal, and it did not occur to her to gather her cloak tightly around her neck or to think of her collarbones. Instead, the fresh fall air blew freely against her skin above her dress, and she walked as if she, too, were free and light as the air. And as each minute passed, she felt freer, lighter, taller.

She had not thought ahead. She had been too busy daydreaming. Too busy enjoying the newly-found freedom of it all to prepare the words to tell her brothers. Her announcement had burst from her like sunshine, like laughter. But the black torment roiling on their faces had preceded a thunderous roar.

"No sister of ours is gonna marry a Mexican!"

Their response was a sudden blow to her soaring spirit. Their immovable mandate shook her, startling her awake from a beautiful dream, and like the suddenly awakened, she was fierce and ill-tempered. "Are you totally INCAPABLE of understanding love?" Their shouts grew, the accusations and objections multiplying.

Afterwards, she would be able to remember very little of it, but they would remember barely too much. At one moment, they even tried to convince her, Willie saying, "What folks in this town gonna think of you, if you livin' with a Mexican? What they gonna say about your children? Your children, *they'd* be Mexican, you know. . . . What they gonna say of *us*?" and Max just ordering, "You ain't gonna do it. THAT's what!"

"I'm going to do what I want! You can like it or not like it, but you will not stop me!"

"You tie up with that greaser, and you not gonna get one piece of this land. This is Steuben Ranch, not *Greaser* Ranch."

"You can have your Steuben Ranch! I'll go to Mexico with him – and you can sit and worry about whether 'the greasers' are coming to take it away!"

"You couldn't! A greaser and a woman? Ha!" Max spit it out like a dirty joke.

In a moment, she was full of disgust. And the thought of leaving, turning, escaping filled her with the breath of cool excitement. To leave behind her brothers – her brothers taking from her, demanding from her, expecting from her, waiting to be waited on. While José – well, José . . . and without warning it came out.

"The two of you together don't make a tenth the man that 'greaser' is."

The brothers were speechless, pale. Riding on her anger, Ilse moved the chair out to the front porch, stepped up and pulled the paper sign from above the door, ripped it and tossed it into the fire, saying, "Try to run this place without me! YOU wear the apron!" She tore her apron off, threw it at them, and went to her room, determined to reclaim her dreams.

Willie and Max had business in town the next day and had to leave the ranch. They left José at the farthest end of the ranch, fixing the fence alone, and said they'd pick him up on their way back that afternoon; that way, they felt sure that nothing would happen. He had wanted to take a jug of water with him, but they said the wagon was too heavy already, and there was a certain pleasure in Max's voice when he joked to Willie, "Maybe he'll die of thirst."

As they were getting near to town, a group of people on Parkerson's porch started laughing, and Willie looked over his shoulder nervously, wondering if they were laughing at them. They couldn't possibly know. Then, a little further along, some greasers were talking in Spanish and lowered their eyes as the Steubens passed – could they know? Were they secretly laughing at him too? Were they planning to move onto the ranch with all their family, like Mexicans do?

Inside the store, Willie made a point to pronounce his English very carefully and to sound in every way like the storekeeper, whose grandfather had constructed most of the few buildings in the town. Max looked over his shoulder, too, whenever he heard a group talking low or laughing. They hurried home, and the ride was unusually hot and stifling, as Max fumed and Willie blushed, both feeling more like strangers in the town than they'd ever felt. Neither their arrival at their ranch nor the setting of the sun seemed to cool them.

At home, the food was on the stove, but Ilse had not served their plates. She came out of her room only once, and when Max sneered "Seen your greaser today?" She turned slowly and let it out like a cutting ice: "No, I haven't seen any men at all today. And I don't see any here now. Perhaps we could ask José to come in and help you run your ranch, since every ranch needs a *man*." Ilse poured her glass of water and went back to her room, as her brothers sat and silently boiled.

Something had to be done before people found out. Max was the one who thought of it really, but from there it kind of hatched on its own. They made their plans, almost without talking, almost without looking at each other's eyes – they walked mechanically, simply, gathering what they needed. They were intoxicated on anger, yet when Willie closed the door behind them early that morning, he did it softly, partly not to wake Ilse, but more because he feared the slamming of the door might jar the two of them to wakefulness, a wakefulness they did not want.

They arrived at the shack softly enough to hear his regular breathing. Then Max brought the plank down over his head, and Willie tied his arms. It was cold in the fields, and hard to carry the kicking wetback, who'd come to sooner than they'd hoped, but they wanted to run as quickly and quietly as possible. For all their anger, they did not want her to see. The wetback was making too much noise and fighting too hard, so they stopped short of their original destination, knocked him one to the jaw, threw the kerosene from the lamp towards his lean body, and lit the match.

Ilse woke with a start. Some scream inside her had jarred her sleep. Through the window she saw figures in the fields, figures that even in her sleep were frighteningly too familiar. Then she heard the screams. And as the sudden cold fear rose through her chest, she whipped to her feet and tore through the door. She shot across the fields, past the tiny, wooden shack, and out to that distant fire dancing in the fields.

The blazing man ran on stumbling half-feet in one long tearing shout that would not stop. She arrived in time to see José running, ablaze, and then stop, his eyes on her, and fall to the ground, face forward, in silence. She ran to grab him but her brothers pulled her away from the burning body. Ilse shook them off like poisonous vines and fell to the ground, taking up his long throaty scream and sobbing there till the sun finally came up.

<hr />

The next morning, Daniel Ibarra answered the knocking at his door to find the Méndez boys trembling and out of breath. Their eyes were immense, swollen, scared to tell what they had seen from a distance last night. They had been walking to town, to their *tía's* house, hoping she could help with the screaming, colicky baby, when they saw what they could hardly believe.

Daniel was in shock. He could only absorb. Then he nodded, and they knew he would do something about it and left, feeling somehow protected. As Daniel turned, he saw his eldest daughter staring at him, eyes wide and face pale. Then she burst, ran to the bed, and cried and cried, something he realized he had not seen her do in three years.

Ibarra gathered his coat, closed the door quietly behind him, and started down the long road to town. He had always had better luck with the *gringos* than did his friends. Maybe it was because his lighter skin (*perlado*, his grandma had called him at birth) made it easier for them to see him as being like them – a little. Maybe it was his ability to read and write English – which many of the *gringos* could not – or to interpret the once-a-year correspondence they received in Spanish. He was sure the sheriff would listen.

Daniel stood, hat in hand, facing the sheriff. He had told all he knew, and the sheriff had averted his eyes. Finally, Sheriff Mill looked at him and said, "What proof you got this happened?"

"We have the witnesses, sir, and the body – what's left of it – should still be on the ranch."

"But how do I know this Ho-zay Silva exists? You got papers?"

"But he was a *mojado*, sir. You remember, he worked at the Steubens' place."

"I don't know of any illegals in this town. . . . Need papers to show a man existed. Can't murder a man that never lived. . . . You bring me the papers – 'til then, weren't no murder took place."

And the sheriff stood up and adjusted his gun belt, a sign that the conversation was over.

At home, Dia was already dressing the straw doll for bed and covering him with his sheet, a crumpled paper she had found today. On the straw doll's leafy pillow, she laid the tiny mesquite blooms she had gathered, and at his feet, the cracked pieces of a sparrow's egg.

Fifty years later, the story would still be told among the *mexicanos* of that place, in late-night whispers by the fire. Their low voices would re-tell how the two brothers had died, one six years later, and one eight, consumed by silence and overwork. How no one had ever worked for them again. And how Elsa would sit in her night gown, blanket in her lap, rocking on her porch, year after year, staring out at the fields, as if she were looking at someone who didn't exist.

Invisible

She was ugly. Or worse, plain. Nothing that nobody could even dress up to be other than plain. She could enter a room and no one would even look up. She could walk past a crew of construction workers at lunchtime and no one would even look past their sandwich. Not even Mama's friends would tease like they did to other mothers, "Ooh, has this baby grown!" or "What happened to *you*? When'd YOU get all grown up, girl?" They never even mentioned her at all, just accepted the iced tea Mama had asked her to bring them and looked right past her.

Dark, round face, unremarkable bare eyes, one and the same color spread over skin, eyes and lips, the only comment she'd ever received on her looks was a casual "*Media trompuda*" from her mother, commenting on her lips and teeth protruding a bit too far. The clear-cot translation she could give it in English was "a little too much snout." Even when her figure filled out, and her breasts had filled the brassiere cups, no one noticed.

Sometimes, as a young teen, she had stood on the edge of the bathtub, perched high enough to be able to see her body reflected in the mirror above the sink. She struggled to maintain her balance, worried about the noise a fall would cause, but she was determined to see herself. With the door locked and all her clothes removed, she studied the mirror. She saw strange (and ugly, she thought) nuances against smooth brown skin. Dark, curly hair growing in a big bush where it most embarrassed her; dark, bumpy circles, too big, around the tips of the mis-shaped breasts; and then, four too-skinny limbs sticking out from a too-fat torso. Still, while she studied all the fragments at length, it was difficult to see the whole. Perhaps the fault was the mirror's. It was not really large enough. Or perhaps, the fault was her own. She was not really visible enough. So she resigned herself, hoping maybe something would bloom in her face or her body or her overall appearance as she grew older.

She got a job, waitressing at the drugstore lunch counter, but people never saw her. They gave their orders to her notepad, not to her.

Just once, she thought someone had noticed her. A man sat quietly in the corner booth. He was older than the teenage boys she studied from a distance at school, and older than the young-to-mid-20's delivery men she studied at a distance from the door to the back parking lot. His long, curly lashes framed the dark shine of his eyes as his gaze poured into the book in front of him. The scent of a subtle but delicious men's cologne spilled flirtatiously out of the crisp white shirt collar, open at the neck. A glimpse of his brown chest was visible above the "V" of the first fastened button. He was not extraordinarily handsome, could maybe even be considered to have a hint of average, but still he was very classy.

He had ordered routinely, efficiently, and returned his gaze to the book. But later, as she took an order from the adjacent booth, he had raised his head and stared, deeply, hungrily, steadily in her direction, as the hint of a smile curled up at the corners of his full lips. The slow, deep dreaminess of his gaze had caught her by surprise; the fullness of the now-parted lips had carried too much sensuality to ignore; his look stole her breath away.

She blushed, stumbled a bit, as she left the booth and headed for the counter, to leave off the order. His head was still raised, his gaze still deep, but his eyes had not moved when she did. She could see now that they were focused on nothing in this room. They were in a dream, a memory maybe, a thought, and eventually, they returned to the book, the same smile on the corner of his lips now directed at the small black letters on the cream-colored page.

She stopped, reached deep into her belly to find a breath of air, slumped into a restrained sigh, and lowered her eyes, demoting herself back down to where she, just five minutes ago, had never doubted she belonged: in the emptiness of a mirror with no reflection, a shadow without a face.

The classy man with the full lips gestured for a ticket, and she took it to him. Avoiding the shine in his eyes, she placed the ticket on the counter and mumbled "Thank you" quickly as she made her getaway.

At school, she did her work, passed her classes, listened to the girls gossip about what different boys had said to them, or tried to do to them. Some of them lied, she knew, claiming they had done things they hadn't, or claiming they had *not* done things they had. Still, even the ugliest of the girls had had *someone* do or say *something*, even if it was nasty or uncaring or just using them. Some had been made fun of by someone saying they loved the ugliest guy in class and laughing real loud afterward. Even that would have been something. But she was *worse* than ugly, she concluded. She was invisible.

At her graduation, she crossed the stage, wondering if people saw an empty cap and gown walk across, or just nothing at all. It was the latter, she decided, since anything she put on would disappear right with her. The principal mispronounced her name and the Superintendent of Schools missed her hand on the handshake, correcting the mistake with a brief touch of the fingertips before the next graduate approached.

She increased her hours at the drugstore. Sometimes, people forgot to tip. Occasionally, when business was slow, she would walk over to the Hair Brushes & Accessories Aisle, and stare at her face in the $5.99 large hand-held mirror. She never took it off the rack, just dipped her face down enough to look into it. After a while, she quit seeing anything.

One day, her six-year-old niece came over to read "Grandma" her new book. "I want to read it again, Grandma!" said Cindy. The telephone rang and Grandma had to take it. So she alone was left to listen to Cindy's performance. Cindy didn't hide her disappointment. "Just You??? Hmph!" The second reading was conducted as if to an empty audience.

"The Ugly Duckling!" Cindy announced, reading each page with flair and importance. When Cindy finished, she turned to leave, not expecting even applause from this unimpressive non-audience, but the young girl was surprised to hear an audience comment.

"It lied," came the flat but quiet voice out of her mouth. "It lied. The ugly duckling doesn't become a swan. It becomes an ugly, grownup duck." Cindy looked like she was about to break out crying for a moment, but then it passed, and she left the room haughtily, smirking "You don't know nothing anyway."

Alone after the young child's exit, she spent the rest of the evening doodling. Things that looked like ugly ducks marched across the page, invisibly, quacking inaudible quacks. One wore a cap and gown, another a waitress frock, another a housedress, another a low-cut nightgown. She felt like something inside her was going to break.

The next day was Friday and it was her day off. She spent it wandering the streets downtown, staring into shop windows, watching couples walk past, lingering in front of the construction sites, standing in front of the beauty shops. She bought a magazine, and for hours that night, turned the pages, searching the faces of the beautiful young models, searching for what feature they possessed that gave them that beauty, or what feature they did not possess that allowed them to be so different from her.

By Saturday, she had scheduled an appointment for a makeover at the best makeup counter at the mall. But when it was done, no one noticed, not even people who knew her. Nothing had changed. If anything, she felt even more invisible, camouflaged now behind this wall of makeup. It had failed.

On Sunday, she cut models' faces out of the magazine and pasted them over her hand-held mirror. Then, she pasted them all over the mirror of her dresser. By the time she realized what she was doing, there was no space left on the mirror big enough to even see an eye. She sat down on the bed and cried dry, empty, invisible tears.

On Monday, she went through work in a daze. She felt she was so invisible, so "not there" that one day she would surely go up in an unnoticed wisp of smoke, disappearing altogether. Or perhaps, she would explode in one long, loud scream that would break all the mirrors and windows of the drugstore. The latter turned out to be a pleasing thought, and she even smiled a moment before telling her boss she was sick and had to go home. She went straight to bed, closing her eyes to try to shut out all her ugliness. But the ugliness kept swirling, sweeping over her like a tornado, erasing everything in its path.

On Tuesday, the classy-looking man with the delicious scent came in again. After taking him his plate, she surprised him (and herself) by turning right around and coming back to his table, facing him squarely and saying in a voice firm and flat, "I think you're very good looking." He was taken aback, had no answer, but then she expected none. She expected nothing. But when she left his table, she was surprised to notice a new feeling washing over her, a feeling more powerful and visible than she had had in years.

She remembered that feeling all week, and it made the air she breathed feel cooler, go deeper, and somehow, leave her a little intoxicated. Then, on Thursday, without knowing it was coming, she did something crazy again. She told an older lady nervously buying arthritis-pain formula at the cash register, "I like your smile." The old lady stopped abruptly, searched her eyes hungrily, and finally smiled again, this time a slow, intimate smile like the kind you give friends you've known a long time. The old lady walked out taller, less lonely, and somehow, at the cash register, she felt less lonely as well.

By Saturday, she had given seven customers, two deliverymen, and three strangers on the street tangible proof that they had been seen. Some shucked off the compliments, others looked surprised, many smiled and said thank you. By the next week, it had taken on all the fiery furor of a campaign, and business at the drugstore lunch counter had picked up. A mad craze had possessed her, and she didn't care who thought what of it. It felt more real and visible and magical than anything she'd felt in all her life.

"Your hands move very gracefully."

"You look like you're carrying a lot of responsibilities."

"Are you sure you want the soup of the day? You look unde-cided."

"You dressed with a lot of style today."

"Have you been working out? You look more muscular."

"Your eyes are shining today."

She even talked the manager into letting her tape a small hand mirror to the cash register with a sign that said "You're one of Our Favorite Customers!"

"That way everybody can see themselves as an important part of our business," she had rationalized to him. The truth of it was - she just wanted them to see themselves.

By the end of the summer, word was out in town, and the drug-store lunchcounter had become something of a trendy hangout. She had moved rapidly from "the waitress who knows everybody" to "Hey, uh, I'm sorry, what's your name?" to "Juana the Waitress" to "Juana" or for those who spoke no Spanish, "Wanna." She was always early to arrive at the lunchcounter, but often people were there already, waiting for her, waiting to see what she would say to them.

"You look pensive...profound. Got a lot on your mind?"

"You've got that courageous King-of-the Jungle strength about your shoulders today."

"What a wonderfully gentle look on your face. You must be a very kind person."

It must have been about five months later when one of the guys asked her out, but she was so surprised by it, she didn't even take it seriously. By the time the year had passed, several of the customers had asked her out, but since her work hours had increased, it seemed no one could ever get a yes. One day, the quiet classy guy came in without a book. He ordered easily, used to the comfortable banter that now routinely flowed between almost all of the customers in the drugstore.

"So how are you doing, Juana?"

"Fine. Hey, I like that blue shirt on you - it really brings out the ruddy glow in your cheeks," she said casually.

"Naw, I like the white better on him," said the guy in the next booth, leaning over to grab a few more lines of conversation with Juana, "Blue looks better on someone like me, *que no*? Brings out MY ruddy glow more than his, right, Juana? The guys in the booth with him laughed at his obviousness.

"Hey, Juana, when you gonna marry me?" the intruding customer continued. "I'm a good prospect, and a real HOT PROPERTY!"

"Well, hot anyway," teased one of his friends.

The classy guy, whose name she'd learned long ago was Arturo, followed her movements obviously, with a gaze both intimate and far-away. Every time she passed near his booth, his full lips parted, as if he wanted to speak, but as she moved on to the other tables, the sensual lips closed again, saying nothing. Finally, the bulk of the lunch crowd had thinned out. She came back by Arturo's booth, asking if he cared for another cup of coffee or a dessert.

"So why don't you go out with these guys? They keep asking you."

"I'm too young to get serious," she laughed, and changed the topic. "Are you combing your hair differently? I like it."

"Tell me the truth, Juana. I've never heard you say yes to them. *No seas mala*, tell me straight. Are you seeing somebody?"

Juana picked up his tip from the table and sighed a long, deep grin directly at him. The answer she would give him later would require much more than a yes or a no. She carried the plates in her hand back to the kitchen. On the way, she passed the mirror on the cash register, saw her face, and smiled.

The Stuff to Scream With

I don't scream. I ain't never been able to scream. Guess God didn't give me the voice. I just do what I tol most the time, take care of the kids, and don't bother nobody else. I stay quiet like you're sposed to.

Once, I tried. I was little. My older cousin Manda, she tol me, "Can't you scream, *muchacha*?" I shook my head. She said, "Here, do it. I take you someplace where nobody else can hear you. Then, you do it." So she took me. Behind the neighbors' garage. Next to the empty lot, where we used to throw mudballs at the wall and no one could see us. Then she said, "Go head." I opened my mouth and made a sound, but it sounded like someone else's sound, like someone else's voice someplace else.

She said, "Girl, that ain't no scream." She stared at me, studying, daring me, then just figuring. She screamed at the top of her lungs. I looked around, scared we'd get scolded. But we didn't. 'Cause there was nobody there to scold us. She screamed again. Loud! She screamed a third time, louder this time than all the other screams, an' long. An' I didn't know why, but I smiled. She smiled too. Then she just looked at me, like waiting.

"I can't," I said. "I don't have the stuff to scream with."

"Everybody gots the stuff to scream with. If you can talk, you can scream. Maybe even if you can't talk, you can scream. Try. You'll see."

I wanted to tell her I can't, you know, but she looked at me so hard, her eyes so much like two black knives that can cut you, that I opened my mouth and pushed out the breath, all funny-sounding and low and full of air. But it sounded like a sound. It didn't sound like a scream.

"Try again," she said. "Jus do it. Thinka the scary movies."

An I thought of those ladies that let out those screams in the movies, like everybody turns aroun an' you hear it real, real cutting through like something more than speaking, more than singing, more like from inside you, and more important than any other sound aroun. An' I wanted, an' I opened my mouth an' – well, something came out but it sounded silly, like a shout high up and too quiet, like someone acting in a school play that lets out a sound in a way they not sposed to.

She was lookin at me so hard an' with a frown so down that I opened my mouth again, without her even tellin me to. But then I closed it, cause I didn't know what to do, an' I didn't want to make that funny sick sound again for both of us to hear.

"I can't."

Then Manda said, "Jus do it."

Then Manda took her strong hands and her zig-zaggy finger-nails and grabbed up a piece of my stomach like you would grab a piece of bread that you were going to tear offa the *bolillo*. An' she pulled and twisted and tried to tear off that piece of my skin. I sucked in the air an' it made a sound, but the sound didn't go out, like a scream. It jus wen in, like a loud breath. I was scared, cause Manda'd never tried to hurt me before, an' I was feelin hurt too, cause I'd always liked her before that. Finally I whined a little quiet "Ow-w-w-w" an' she let go.

Then she just sat down on the old bricks thrown on the ground, an' put her head on her fists. I stood there, scared to say anything, an' my eyes stinging from the red and purple-white stripes on the skin above my shorts. After a while, I realized that she wasn't mad at me, so I sat down too, an' wiped the muddy streaks of *mocos* and tears away.

"Don't you want to hit me or anything?" she asked, all gentle-like. I shook my head. "You can scream real loud now if you want to," she said, more soft now than I'd ever heard her talk, almost like she was asking me somethin, like to have a cookie or somethin.

We jus sat there, with the weeds taller'n both of us. We sat there a long while, until my breathing was real slow again an' the muddy streaks on my face were dry. Then she reached in her pocket an' got out a gingerbread *marranito*. Jus a crumbly half of one, like the head and maybe three legs. (It didn't have its bottom anymore, like she'd probably been eating it all day for snacks, little at a time.) An' she took the whole thing, not just a part of it, an' she tore it in half an' gave me half. I guess she felt bad that she'd cut me an' I hadn't even gotten a scream for it. An' we ate it slow together an' all quiet.

So, see? Even Manda knows that I don't scream. An' Manda's smart on those things. But everytime I'd see her after that, she'd always look at me real quiet at first, like almost mad, an' then we'd go on, jus normal, playing an' talking an' stuff. But at the end, before she'd leave, she'd always hit me one good, like when no one was looking. But I never screamed, not even then.

An' we wen on an' growed up. An' every once in a while, like at Tía's house making *tamales* or at my folks' place, when I'd see her, she'd ask, "You ever learn to scream yet?" An' I'd jus look at her, an' she'd turn away, knowin the answer. An' jus once, when we were at Gramma Salazar's house, she sat next to me while I was watching *The Price is Right* an' some lady was screaming every time Bob Barker said what was the prizes they were giving away. An she said to me, "You got the scream inside you. I know. All you need's the way to get it out."

But Manda moved to someplace in California, like Fresno or something, after she got married, an' I don't hardly see her anymore. An' most the time, everything's real quiet, an' I just do what my husban says, an' most times there's no trouble. The kids are growing an' Raul's almost as tall as Armandita now, with the baby not far behind now that he's walking.

An' my neighbor she screams all the time. Sometimes I just sit an' watch her, from my porch. She has five kids, so it's always "*Ay-y-y!* The baby's gonna fall off the high chair!! *Ay-y-y!* Juanito's in the shoe polish!! *Ay-y-y!* Maria's playing basketball in the street *y a'i viene una trocota – Ay-y-y!* I can hear it com-m-i-i-i-ing!!" An' Jose Raúl, my huuban, calls her "*La Lucuratalosa*" an' he comes home from work an' says, "Can you turn the TV up a little? It's after supper so she's gonna start now, *ya va a comenzar La Escandalosa.*" An' I smile.

But this morning I took my kids to the park, an' we were having a good time. Raulito an' Armandita on the swings an' the baby in the sand box, *to'o contentito,* full of sand an' throwing it around like it was water! Then I look back at the swing an' Raulito was going real high but okay, an' Armandita's swing was empty. An' I look at the slide an' I look at the water fountain an' I look at the see-saw an' she wasn't there. An' my heart it goes up in my mouth like it gonna fly out an' I grab the baby, sand an' all an' start running all around, like in circles, in an' out of bushes an' trying to go all over the park at the same time, not knowing which way first and shouting to Raul, "Stay on the swing! Stay on the swing! Don't go nowheres! NOWHERES!!"

I run to the fence by the big trees, then the side o the bathroom, then behind the bathroom.

An then I find Him in the bushes, his old, white hand on his dirty pants zipper an' a lollipop in the other hand, an' him saying 'Sh–

sh" an smiling ugly at Armandita. An' her looking up at the lollipop, all different colors swirled together like the kind she always asking for at the grocery store, but they 79 cents each and we get the little ones, one flavor, that are twelve for a dollar. And the "Sh-sh" rumbles through my ears loud like a bulldozer, with the engine breathing through me, and then the engine explodes.

An before I know what I'm gonna do, I knock him down an' hit his hands with that big rock. I donno when I got the rock or when I put down the baby, but I jus keep hitting his hand till I smash that lollipop all to little pieces of color you can't see no more. An' I can hear myself breathin hard, with each time I hit with the rock. An' I can feel him twist an' moan an' try to get away, but I on him hard an' heavy an' he can't go nowhere an' I say, "Scream! Scream! Scream! SCRE-E-EAM!!!" And from somewhere far away, long away, I hear –

. . . I scared, Daddy. I scared. No, you not. I hurt, Daddy. I hurt.

No, you don'. I no want to. Pl-e-ease, I no want to. Sh-sh-sh - be quiet. Go sleep, I won't hurt you. Sh-sh, do this for Daddy, okay? Do what Daddy wants, okay? *Cáyate, huerca,* cut out that crying *o te doy un paletazo.* But I wan- na cry - it hurts! You don't know what hurts - Quit crying or I'll give you something to really cry about.

Sh-sh-ta! Nothing hurts. Just *cáyate!* Chut up!! It DON'T HURT!!

If you scream, I'll . . .

The tears an' the *mocos* were coming out of me like water, like a *río* so full an' flowing bubbly, while I whisper, "Scream! Scream!!!" An' then I hear a scream, a long, terrible, deep scream, like years long and hurts loud. A with-all-the-stuff-it's-got scream. An' then I see Armandita looking at me, all surprised, her eyes real open. An' a crowd of people all aroun starin at me. An' I look down an' see this ole man, all *barbudo* an' ole clothes an' half-drunk maybe, I donno.

An' I think, José Raul's gonna get mad at me, beatin up this ole man. An' the ole man, he looks bad, so I get off an' leave him there. An' I take Armanda by one hand an' the baby by the other, an' I walk to the swings where Raulito is still going so high, so fast, an' I walk all three of 'em all the way to the store, where I get Armandita one of those lollipops with lots of colors like she say she want. Jus the way she want. With her voice. Her voice strong that don't ever gonna be shut up. By nobody.

I Just Can't Bear It

Jimmy López was the kind of man everybody knew would have lots of people at his funeral, and you knew there were gonna be lots of nice things said about him from the altar and all. In fact, you knew that the people would start showing up in large bunches even at the "Visitation" at Angeles Funeral Home. So his wife made sure to get her hair dyed even before the "viewing" at the funeral home. Then her sister-in-law helped her put cold cucumber slices over her eyes that morning, so the puffiness would go down a little. But that day, it didn't seem to help much.

And sure enough, just as expected, people who'd voted for him as well as those who'd voted against started showing up to shake their heads, cover their mouths, whisper a few complimentary stories to the people beside them and, of course, work their way slowly to the widow's side, at an available moment, and offer an *abrazo*, a handshake or a *pésame*.

"*Le doy mi pésame,*" (I offer to you that I share your pain) said several of the *comadres*. "What a tragedy for us all," said several of the important business people. "He was a model citizen...a pride to our race," hyperventilated Mike Gomez, who hoped to replace him in the next election for school board. "Mr. Low-pezz will be hard to replace," pontificated the Anglo school board president who had been shocked at the rumor two years ago that a SECOND Mexican-American might run for and be part of the ten-member board.

One by one they floated toward the front pew, where Jimmy's wife sat, eyes dazed and makeup odd and clownlike, she had concluded this morning as she stared blankly at the mirror. The sounds of praise and mourning seemed to rise and wane, like gentle ocean waves in the distance, rolling forward in "Ohs" and "Ahs" and then receding in quiet, respectful whispers, punctuated by the seafoam of sniffles.

Visitors also whispered to each other, each trying to pay their rightful dues for having outlived him. "He was so well respected. Even the one-armed man who sells apples in front of the courthouse came, and sat quietly in the back row for almost twenty minutes! They say

Jimmy once gave him money for medicine."

Sometimes their stories built on each other's, each trying to be more complimentary than the preceding.

"If Jimmy hadn't been Mexican," the town mechanic sighed, "he'd a probably been a City Councilman!"

"No, *compadre*," countered back the owner of El Sombrero Mexican Restaurant, his eyebrows raising in self-importance and his eyes assuming that hunt-for-a-big-enough-exaggeration look they all recognized, "if Jimmy hadn't been Mexican, he'd a made it all the way to Mayor!"

There was not a soul in the room who did not shake his head and express sorrow at Jimmy's passing. Occasionally, someone would sob, more often they would just sigh, but it was a very, very nice gathering.

"AY, I JUST CAN'T BEAR IT!" the shout cut the room. "I CAN'T BEAR TO SEE HIM!" screamed the inconsolable bawler in the back row.

Somehow the rhythm of ocean waves was broken.

"NO! NO! NO! HE JUST CAN'T BE DEAD!"

Every eye was trying to strain their peripheral vision backward, while the torsos were frozen in polite postures. Neck muscles strained, and a few uninhibited souls turned clear around to study the face of the woman who was in such pain. People blinked their eyes, lowered their heads, and tried to keep their thoughts, or at least their body language, focused on their mourning, but the sobbing screams of the woman made it hard to maintain their pose.

"I CAN'T BELIEVE IT! I CAN'T BELIEVE IT! NO, THIS IS TOO MUCH TO BEAR! THIS IS JUST –"

Within seconds, a chain of questions had been passed through them, via eyebrows and wide eyes, clenched jaw muscles and twisted mouths, but no one seemed to know who she was. They scanned their memories, trying to place a distant niece or a cousin's child, perhaps even a loyal worker whose crisis he'd resolved, but no one came to mind. No one even faintly recognized her, and they could not even pretend to pretend that she was a distant cousin.

"—TERRIBLE! I CAN'T BEAR TO SEE HIM LIKE THIS."

By now, even the widow had turned around to study the face, with her lips all screwed together and an out-of-patience look in her dead-serious eyebrows.

"I CAN'T TAKE IT! I JUST CAN'T GO ON! –"

The out-of-patience look in the widow's eyes had been replaced by an I'm-gonna-kill-her look.

"AY! AY! QUE TRISTEZA! SE ME QUIEBRA EL –"

Most of the faces at the funeral were easily familiar, but some had taken a while to identify, as information was passed from one person to the next. People assumed most of the unfamiliar ones were business associates of his, or friends from different circles, perhaps even different towns. Mr. Lopez often traveled to nearby burgs or all the way to San Antonio for what he always said were "very important meetings," although some had whispered that he could more easily enjoy the bars where he was not as well known or as quickly recognized. "He did like his cups," said one man, with a half-smile. "Have to admit he knew how to enjoy life," said another, "and had a great eye for women..."

"—CORAZÓN! TELL ME IT'S NOT TRUE!"

"There was one time we crossed over to Piedras Negras, when we were young, just into our forties, and—" the man was cut off by a jab from his wife.

"AY, NO PUEDO! NO PUEDO CON ESTE –"

The bawler didn't even stop for breath, but just ran one scream into another, each one louder and more dramatic than the previous. There WERE a few *comadres* in town that were heavy criers at the funerals (one had even threatened to throw herself in the grave when her first husband passed away), but this lady surpassed anything they had ever witnessed from a non-spouse, non- . . . "Well," they thought, "we'd better not even say it."

"DOLOR! I JUST CANNOT BEAR IT! I JUST CANNOT BEAR IT."

The school board president had already scooted out, mumbling something about an important meeting, and Mike Gomez was casting nervous glances at the door, trying to figure how to exit gracefully. The El Sombrero owner just shook his head rapidly and mumbled, "Well, some secrets never come out 'til the grave..."

The lady who did Jimmy's wife's hair every Saturday was whispering to her neighbor, "You know, one time I saw him driving out of town and I just KNEW that something suspicious was –"

The widow had had enough. She stood in a motion so slow and powerful it drew an unintended gasp from the crowd. She moved to the front of the room, body slanted only partially to the coffin, but eyes focused in a threatening slant to the back of the room. She addressed the dear aggrieved slowly, word by carefully chosen word, in a voice both calm and booming:

"Our . . . sorrow . . . is . . . overwhelming. Our words . . . cannot. . . . express. We cannot bear . . . the sad farewell. But – GOODBYE, JIMMY!" she announced loudly as she slammed down the lid of the coffin.

The ears of the mourners were blasted with a sound louder than the coffin closing: the ringing sound of sudden silence. The bawler had stopped her bawling. The bawler, her eyes spread to two long ovals, had dropped open her mouth.

"Jimmy?" she asked blankly.

"This is Jimmy? You mean this is not Chemo? Chemo Carrizales? I was positive she said yes when I asked at the door if this was for Chemo."

Then she rose from her seat, saying simply, "It's not Chemo," and walked out. Only the people in the back two rows heard the mumble as she moved down the hall, "Who the hell is Jimmy?"

Everyone stared at each other openly, the corners of their eyes not quite yet ready to crinkle in the asking of permission to giggle.

In fact, the giggling had only begun to spill forth when from down the hall in a different "Visitation" room came the familiar wailing:

"AY, I JUST CAN'T BEAR IT! I JUST CAN'T BEAR TO SEE HIM!"

The volcano of laughter had begun to erupt, but everyone, even Jimmy, knew that Jimmy's "Visitation" for that day was over.

How I Got Into Big Trouble
and the Mistakes I Made,
in increasing order of importance

for Barbara, who lived it

MISTAKE #1:
First, I fell in love with my priest. That was enough right there, but then I made Mistake # 2.

MISTAKE #2:
I told my parents that I fell in love with my priest. (My parents got very mad.)

MISTAKE # 3:
I told my priest that I fell in love with my priest. He already knew. Told me he was in love with me, too. (My parents told me it was all my fault.)

MISTAKE # 4:
We tried to figure out a way to make it work. Asked the Church if he could leave the priesthood to get married. Waited for permission. They didn't give it. He left anyway, and we got married by a judge. (My parents quit talking to me.)

MISTAKE #5:
Asked the church what we could do to have a full church wedding. They said it wasn't possible. Asked if they could at least give the marriage their blessing. They said it wasn't possible. Asked if they could give a sorta, kinda half-blessing. Asked every week for eight months solid, and finally they figured out a way. But we had to promise to tell no one, and the church records were sealed in confidentiality. Got our half-blessing. (My parents said that nineteen-year-old "*muchachas*

locas" should never be allowed in the congregations of thirty-year-old attractive single priests. I just shrugged my by-then-pregnant shoulders and said I didn't know any priests who *weren't* single. They ignored me.)

MISTAKE # 6:
We kept thinking we needed to "do the right thing" and be married fully in the eyes of the church. The church made us fill out a thousand forms and talk to a hundred officials and make 10,000 separate vows, including that we would never tell anyone. We didn't. Except for my parents. (My parents started talking to me again. But probably just because their one-year-old granddaughter was already part of the wedding party.)

MISTAKE#7:
Tried to celebrate our anniversary. We had had, by then, three different wedding dates and two children. The children were a lot less confusing than the wedding dates. One of the weddings had been so secret that we couldn't even remember the date of it anymore. Oh well. Happy Anniversary anyway. Whenever it is. (My parents at least agree that he's a very good man. They've *always* loved their priest. It's me that they're not sure about.)

MISTAKE # 8:
He tried to find a job. It's not that he didn't have talents galore. It's just that I kept asking, "Well, what would you like to do?" and what he "would like to do" was be a priest. Manager of a K-Mart couldn't compare. For three years after I'd finished my nursing degree, he was even a househusband. Did a great job and the kids were delighted. He even sewed up down jackets on the sewing machine, and re-paneled the den! But underneath, he knew it was a job on a "mommy-track" and a sure-thing-dead-end once they graduated.

MISTAKE# 9:
They graduated. He turned to drink. Lots of it. Just beers in social settings to start with, but sopping drunk fogouts sprawled on the living room couch at the end. I'd get home from work and they'd get home from college, and the smell of wine would hit us at the front door. Just reliving the transubstantiation of Christ in communion over and over,

I guess. (My parents started patting me on the back, saying things like "Be strong, *m'ija*" and lighting candles for me.)

MISTAKE# 10:
I went to church. Heard a sermon about the evils of over-indulgence and the selfishness of intoxication. Got tired of never being able to use my living room couch. Told my parents that I was getting a divorce. (They put out their candles and decided to quit trying to understand me; maybe I was just *born* bad.)

MISTAKE # 11:
No. No more. Quit counting. This is my life. Come on, I'm serious. I married a patient of mine. Wonderful man, with a kind heart. Kind heart, but weak heart. In fact, he was waiting for a heart transplant. We didn't even *try* for the church. Married in the hospital where I work. He was still in the hospital bed. Signed two pieces of paper, and just take the marriage and go. But this time, I remember my anniversary with NO problem. And we celebrate it. Every month.

("*M'ija*, that man could die at any minute. You're making a big mistake.")
"No, *Mamá*. No more mistakes. I'm the judge, I'm the jury, I'm the church, and I'm giving *me* a full blessing!"

Federico y Elfiria

Pos, he liked her jus' 'cause of that – *no le hacía* – that she was *muy ranchera* and had never seen beyond the walls of her *casa*. She was a good girl, which is like saying that she wasn't a bad girl, not even a little bad, y'know?

The first time Federico started liking Elfiria was the day Chato and Manuel were teasing him and said that Federico was dressing *muy galán*, that a *lo mejor* he was trying to impress the girls. And then Manuel said that a *lo mejor* there was somebody he was already talking to a *las escondiditas*, and Chato (to impress Manuel) said he'd seen Elfiria writing notes with big hearts that said "Federico plus Elfiria." They both laughed a lot at Federico, and Federico got red. He knew that a *lo mejor* Chato was just making it up but *de todos modos*, he wondered. I mean, it was real embarrassing. I mean, Elfiria was the kind of girl that didn't "like" nobody – she just went home from school and did what her parents said. And she wasn't the kind of girl that anyone went around "liking" either. I mean she was just somebody who sat in that desk and whose name got called two before his on the roll, and that's the only way anyone thought of her, y'know? But just the same, he wondered.

And I mean, she'd never had any boyfriends or anything, and you knew she was a good girl (which is to say, not a bad girl).

Well, the next day, Manuel and Chato were talking about the baseball game with Concho Mines High and wondering were they gonna lose now that Pato had signed up for the Air Force and didn't have his mind on baseball anymore, and they had forgotten all about the love notes and the teasing. Federico remembered, but he wasn't gonna say anything. And then he started noticing how Elfiria always had her hair so neatly braided in a *trenza*, and none of the hairs ever loose, and it always fell right down the middle of her back, between her rounded shoulders. Well, he didn't know for certain if they were rounded, but he'd read something like that once, and they looked kind of round since she was *media llenita*, you know. But that was okay because everybody always made fun of guys that went with girls that were *flacas* and called them "Bone Chompers" and things like that. And I mean, nobody was gonna call her "*La Gorda*" of the class 'cause that was María de los Socorros, and there were lots of others almost as fat. Besides, good girls were supposed to be a little *llenita* so they wouldn't look like those *mujeres* in the movies who were definitely *not* good girls.

Still, he wondered. And once, when he was home alone and no one was looking, he drew a little heart (in the corner of an old home-work paper that he was going to throw away) and wrote "Federico + Elfiria" on it. And looked at it, just to see what it looked like (if she had done it, which she probably hadn't, 'cause she was a good girl.) And he liked the way Elfiria had an *F* and an *R* in it, just like Federico. And he noticed how, when the teacher had them check each other's papers, she made her *F*'s kinda nice and open, even when they were *F*'s on somebody's paper. And then one day, Elfiria started looking at him. (Yeah, he looked at her lots, but he only did it when he was sure she didn't see, so it couldn't be that.)

Then *llegó* summer. And Manuel got married. Y Chato *se fue al* Air Force, and at Polos' wedding, Polos laughed and said, "*Ahora sólo quedas tú.* You're the only one left, buddy. What you gonna do?" So he started going to Elfiria's house . . . and after 'while, they got married.

About a year after they were married, he saw this movie. Not *dirty* dirty, *tú sabes*, but it had lotsa good parts in it. He came home all excited. When he came in the door, Elfiria was washing the floor, fac-ing the other way, and her *nalgas* were pointing at him. And *esas cosas* hanging down and jiggling every time she swiped with the sponge. *Pos, que se reventó el globo,* and he was all over her. And him going for her and her fighting him off, kinda (in her feelings), but not saying "no" ('cause she was a good girl and s'posed to let her husband do things like that), and he was real excited, 'cause he knew that's what good girls were s'posed to do (but not do) if they were married. And he started kissing her lots, just kinda forgetting himself. And she even quit making faces for a while. And he was real excited and breathing on her neck hard, like when he – well, you know, did it – an' *pos*, they did, an' just when he was about to – well, you know, *venir* – he just grabbed her neck and kissed it with his teeth and tongue, sucking hard. I don't know why, maybe it was just seeing it in the movie that made him do it, but he didn't do it on purpose. And then he – *pos estaba viniendo* – and she could feel it, you could tell, and she did something that really surprised Federico – she grabbed his head in both her hands and kissed him real hard on the lips.

Well, they were both real sleepy after that and didn't think too much about it that night, but the next day, Federico was still running this over in his head. I mean she'd never acted like that before. (He didn't either, but then he'd seen this love movie, so that was why.) And then he started wondering if maybe she'd seen a movie, too, or something. I mean, she was supposed to be home during the day, and he hadn't heard nothing about her going out to the movies. And this started to get his little hairs on his neck up and prickly until he realized she didn't have no way to get to no movie. And he relaxed.

But then Elfiria got up and started to get dressed, and when she took her robe off, the most horrible thing happened. Right in front of him there was this dark, dark blue mark on her neck and he *knew* what it looked like.

He'd seen those before (at school) but only on bad girls. It looked every bit like a hickey.

And I guess it was okay, what with his being her husband and all, but still – it looked funny and it bothered him. Manuel had always said, "Any girl that lets a guy give her a hickey is *una d'esas*." That night, Federico was still feeling bothered by it and, for some reason, didn't feel like going home right away. I mean he wasn't angry at her or anything, he said, he just wanted to stay out late. After all, he was a man, he could do that if he wanted. It was her business, *cosa de viejas*, staying home. So he went over to the *cantina*. He didn't go in, 'cause he didn't have but forty cents on him, and that was for a Coke to go with his *taquitos* tomorrow lunch, but he still went to the *cantina*, and he parked outside in the *troquita* his brother had given him, and he just watched from the dark. And when it was real late, he went home.

But she was still awake, and that pissed him off. And worse, she was looking at him nice-like, and like she wanted to do something. He just went around the other side of the bed, took off his *zapatos*, and slipped his shirt and pants off quick, leaving his *camiseta* and underwear on. He slipped under the covers, facing the other way and looking asleep.

She was in her gown and she curled up right against him. (*¡Ingrata!* So he could feel her!), and his heart was going double, but he didn't move a muscle, except for squeezing his eyes more shut to look more asleep.

Pos, if *esa ingrata* doesn't squeeze up against him even more, like hinting. And she stays like that, several seconds (or maybe hours), and he's so he can't take it any more and finally – all angry – he shoots off, "*¡Cabrona! ¡Qué* I'm asleep!" And she's so scared, 'cause he's never called her anything like that before, that she doesn't know whether to move away or how, so she just stays absolutely still. And he's so mad that he had to speak that he keeps his eyes even more shut (so she can't say he's awake). And they stay that way the whole night – scrunched up against each other, his eyes squeezed shut, hers scared open, both of them scared to move an inch, and him with a hard-on and her hungry.

Bueno, that kind of did it. I mean, a man can only take so much, you know? I mean, a wife is s'posed to respect him, do what he wants when he wants, and not go bothering him otherwise, y'know?

And for the rest of that week, Federico went to the cantina every evening after work and stayed outside, parked in his *troquita*, came home late and slept in his underwear. And Elfiria went to bed quietly, with her eyes open all night long.

Well, by the end of the week, they both looked pretty bad, but Federico looked the worst. Missing supper and not getting much sleep was really draining him. And Elfiria was lookin' okay, but pretty sad, and never said much – even more so than usual, and she usually didn't say much.

So one day, Federico thought, "Forget the *cantina*, I'm going home for supper." And Elfiria was so surprised, she ran around fixing supper as quick as she could, and they both ate, and without a word, he just went to the bedroom, pulled his clothes off (even his underwear – *¡ya le calaba!*), and went to sleep. She did too. And they slept kinda comfortable. I don't know why, but maybe they were just too tired to care about anything else.

The next day was Saturday and things felt okay. I mean, really quiet, but they did the work they needed to do and then, come evening, ate and Federico went to bed early again. He lay and thought for a while, and wondered about that hickey of Elfiria's, but when she finished the dishes and came to lie down too, he noticed that it had faded almost away, and that made him feel better, so he drifted off to sleep.

Elfiria was really worried about Federico. I mean, she wanted to be a good wife, and she sure didn't like this business of him being angry, so she resolved to try not to do anything to upset him any more. Still, she thought about that one night lots, and how she had felt hot and shivery all over, and she tried not to think about it too much, but she fell asleep thinking about it anyway.

It was maybe 2:00 a.m. and they'd slept for several hours already, when suddenly Elfiria found herself dreaming half-awake and hungry and felt him hard and, just tired of waiting, she pushed herself against him and helped it along. And when Federico woke up, her hand was pushing his mouth against her neck and her – well, all the different parts of her were rubbing up against him, and it all felt real good for about twenty minutes, until he came. And then, he started realizing – well, he wasn't too certain what, but realizing it anyway.

And he looked real quick to see if she had a hickey. And she didn't (or not that he could see in this light, anyway) and that made him feel a little better.

But still . . .

So he fell asleep, but the next day he was worse upset than ever, and made her go to *misa*, while he stayed home and thought. *Pos*, then, if she doesn't up and hit him that week – right in the middle of all his confusion – *con que* she's pregnant. At first, Federico was even more confused – and irritated *que la ingrata* had gone and gotten herself that way right now, when he was trying to figure something else out. But then, when everybody found out, and all the guys patted him on the back and said *que ya era tiempo,* and Polos said his wife was expecting their second, and they all congratulated him, Federico felt pretty good. But still, he wondered. And the next day, he stayed away from work so he could watch the house from behind the bushes, to see if somebody else was coming to visit her.

The sun got pretty hot, *y ya le andaban las moscas* and the dust, but he was determined to find out once and for all if she was a good girl. *Pos,* if he didn't end up staying there *hasta las 2 o'clock de la tarde* and the only thing he saw was that Elfiria hung all his clothes on the line first, and then the *toallas*, and then her clothes. And then she gave the *sobras* from lunch to the neighbor cat. But most of the time, it was just him and the moscas, suffering from the *calor*. At two, he decided she wasn't gonna do anything anymore because that was when she listened to her *novela*, and if she was going to do anything, she wouldn't have made it at that time, 'cause she'd miss "*Amor de Lejos.*" So he decided it was his baby, and, relieved, he left, *sin decirle nada*.

He began to feel real good about her being pregnant, and as she got bigger each month, it made him feel more like one of those *hombres que eran* middle-aged *y bien*-respected. *Y ella se portó bien también, nomás que* around her fifth month she started getting real wet and hungry at night, *e ¡híjole! pregnant y todo, qué desgracia, pero* what could he do? I mean, a man can only hold back so much, and there she was, pushing him to do it!

He didn't like the idea and he didn't agree with it at all – *pero* he was just too tired and turned on to fight it all the time. So, he'd go ahead and do it, and just agree with himself in the morning that it shouldn't be that way, you know, and that it wasn't his fault.

When the time came for him to take her to the hospital, she was screaming and all that woman kind of stuff. Federico tried to be strong for her, but then, as they were walking in the door, she began peeing on the floor, *a chorros*. "Elfa, can't you wait?!" he scolded her in a whisper, embarrassed that the nurses should see his wife letting it all go like that. I guess Elfiria didn't hear him, 'cause she kept right on doing it, and her dress and the floor were all wet. And then he realized it had nothing to do with her going to the bathroom, and the nurse called for a wheelchair, and Federico's stomach felt funny (probably from the leftovers at supper last night), and he slumped onto the check-in counter with a color on his face Elfiria had never seen. For a second, Elfiria forgot her pains and just stared at him in shock, then she caught him just before he went to the floor, and pushed him into the wheelchair, saying to the nurse, "*Cuídamelo.*"

When he came to, she had already been taken in, behind those doors, and the nurse just smiled and said, "We'll let you know when you can go in."

Federico looked at the man in the wheelchair next to him, a *viejito* in his eighties, with an oxygen tube taped to his nose, who said to him, "*Hijo*, what are you in for?" It took Federico a few minutes to comprehend the question, but when he did, he scooted out of the wheelchair as fast as he could. Finally, they let him into Elfa's room, and it was real tough with her screaming and sweating and all, but Federico was real brave about the whole thing.

Sometime around midnight, the doctor came in. He was a yawning old man with a look on his face as if he'd eaten something that didn't taste good. He saw her still in labor and grumbled, half to the nurse and them, and half to his clipboard, "Let's quit all this nonsense and get that baby out. I've got a golf game early tomorrow. She's been in labor seven hours already – prep for a C-section." Federico was about to feel fear coming on when he was interrupted by this loud voice, strangely familiar, yet totally alien.

"¡NO SEÑOR!" It was Elfiria! Talking to the doctor like that! "If you won't help me, then go home and let my mother come!"

⊷⊶

It was a boy. Named after him. Federico was in shock. He'd thought about her being pregnant, but he'd never really thought about the baby. *Su hijo.* Of course he was his – he was named Federico Jr., wasn't he? And when he looked at him for the first time and saw this little person, all alive *y pataleando*, he just said, "I did that?" and melted into a tiny pool of pride and tenderness.

Manuel had come to *acompañarlo.*

"How ya doin' man? *¡Compa'! ¡Papá?!*" Manuel saw Federico's eyes water up as he answered.

"God I feel good."

Manuel, smug over the birth of his own daughter two months earlier, smiled, *muy compañero,* and teased, "You feel good, huh? Oh, and it gets better, *hombre. M'ija 'tá más chula!* And you feel good now? Just wait till Elfiria gets all healed up and starts wanting you again – *¡uy!*" He laughed and nudged Federico. Federico laughed, but only from the face out, *porque* what Manuel had said really bothered him. *Y ni le dieron* the time to absorb that when Elfiria was back in her room and ready for company. . . .

Fred Jr. kept them both so busy that Federico didn't have much time to think about his earlier problems with Elfiria until one day, about seven weeks later, she comes up to him, real *suavecito*-like, y'know, and says, "*Hace mucho tiempo.* I'm healed now, *tú sabes,* down there. . . ." Federico was touched, but, *muy caballero*, comforted her with, "That's okay, honey. I don't need it. I can wait some more."

The dam burst, and Elfiria, tired and glad the baby was finally asleep, burst too. "But *I* need it! *I* can't wait some more!"

Federico was stunned. "But . . . you . . . *¡Hombre!* . . . I always thought you were. . . ." – he gulped and said it directly – "a good girl."

"*¡Ya para con estas tonterías!* Of course I'm a good girl! I'm more than that! *Soy una madre* – the mother of our child – *y soy tu esposa* – wife, you know? Like, married?"

Federico had never thought of it that way. He had always heard of – *pos, tú sabes* – *d' esas*, bad girls, *y también* of course *de* good girls – but of someone being a good girl plus more? Maybe that explained it. Maybe she could be a good girl, plus add on wife and mother, plus add on *more*. He hadn't figured it out completely, *pero* Elfiria interrupted him and said, "*¡Ya olvídate de esas cosas!* Let's go to bed!" And they did, and *pos, tú sabes*, a man can only do so much all by himself.

Waiting Between the Trees

As I drive down the sun-sprinkled path, something between the trees catches my eye. I turn, but there is only a coolness to the air, the edge of excitement, an emotion that leaves its shadow there. Still, I saw it. I know I did. More than a century old but still sprightly and mischievous, hiding between the same two trees. It wasn't mine, but it caught me, and now it is. Mine. It never died.

A dream never does die, really. Even when the person who dreamed it quits believing in it, it doesn't die. Even when lives pass and others take their place, still no death. It just goes out there and sits some place, waiting. Hiding between the trees.

And they're there now. All those little dreams, sitting together, waiting, sometimes for a long, long time. But there – as long as it takes. They are active, growing, hearing everything around them and getting smarter, consorting, consulting, brainstorming, having conventions. Sitting in some spot between two trees. So many of them together that a person just walking through often gets taken, grabbed, embraced, abducted, and adopted by them. Owned, driven.

Watch out. Right behind you. You've got to be careful which one catches you. Watch out!! To your left there – duck! (I wouldn't even go down that path if I were you... it's full of them, you don't stand a chance.)

When mine caught me, it was old, but full of energy. Took my breath away. One minute, things are normal, your life is totally under your control. You think. Next minute, everything's changed. Your whole life has been re-structured, re-directed, revised.

—◆—

"Let's go have a taco together," It dictated, as my car turned to the left suddenly and I found myself pulling into Taco Riendo at the busy hour. I NEVER go to Taco Riendo, but there I was asking "Do you carry guacamole, bean and cheese in a flour tortilla?"

("And two of *carne guisada*," it added. "It's been a long while since I had *carne guisada,* guy. Do they still make it with hand-ground comino like they did ninety years ago?") I wasn't gonna ask them that, no matter what. I'm *tímido*, y'know? Too shy to even say yes when someone at a party asks me if I want a mint or a cookie, even when I want it, much less question a restaurant about how they cook something. I tried to ignore the voice. Mistake.

"Add THREE of *carne guisada* with hand-ground *comino* – from a *molcajete!*" I heard my voice saying, and managed to stifle to a mumble the last tagalong of the interjection, "Don't you guys know ANYTHING of what we learned about spices last century?" It wasn't me talking.

I took a deep breath and shelled out the last of the folded dollar bills from my wallet. So now I had this strange ancient creature talking for me and spending my money to boot.

<hr />

"You *vatos* care for any *carne guisada?*" I heard the voice ask two bloodshot winos sitting on the curb outside. They thanked me profusely and swallowed down the tacos before I could even pocket my meager change, which they also thanked me for.

"So why did you order three tacos if you were gonna give'm away? It's the end of the month and I won't get my paycheck for at least a week!"

"It feels SO good being able to share! It's been a really long while since I shared, too!"

I was ready to feel irritated, but there was something so *cariñoso* about its expression that I found myself fascinated again, almost infatuated with this strange thing riding in the car with me.

"Let's go back to the park," it dictated, "I don't want to get the bends, you know, coming up too soon after all those years. I'd better take it easy. A *carne guisada* taco *and* sharing with the same wino spirits on the same corner as before - it's almost too much. *¡Vámonos!*"

I found myself thinking how glad I was that it spoke Spanish too, until something in the logic part of my brain said, "This doesn't make sense what language it is, since it's just talking to you mentally anyway." Whatever. I was willing to suspend logic for now, just to figure out what was going on emotionally that tasted so good. The taco tasted good too. It was one of those unbelievable spring-in-the-middle-of-winter San Antonio days, and the breeze and the filtered sun were the perfect combination under the pecan trees, as we sat on the soft brown leaves, soaking up the warmth. I finished the taco, took a deep breath, and leaned my head back against the tree trunk, not even caring anymore if I interrogated this thing, not even worrying if it would last or disappear.

"The *comino* wasn't ground in a *molcajete*, but it was freshly ground anyway," the thing dictated to me, quietly.

"SO!" It shook me from my drowsy, sunlight-through-the-trees almost-siesta. "Should we try to get some more people in on this?"

"On what?" I felt like I was in some kind of blatant denial, but I didn't even know what IT had already signed me up for.

"On WHAT? You got a lotta work to do!"

Like I said before, watch out when one gets you, because they don't let go easy, and you kind of get the feeling you're in it for life. And maybe, you are.

Actually, I'm a teacher by training. I got the urge to become a teacher because of radical old books like *Teaching as a Subversive Activity* from the 70's, and wanting to change the world one kid at a time. So after getting my degree I headed back to teach in the same low-income, *barrio* school that I had attended in the days when all the students were Mexican, and all of the teachers were NOT. It didn't pay worth beans, and all the people that had graduated with Business Majors were buying houses and new cars when I was still glad to be paying back my college loans, but hey – I love my job. Besides, some of those business major types have already dropped dead of heart attacks, or gotten divorces and bought motorcycles trying to "find themselves" when I've known where I live for a long time already. Still, with laws that push state-mandated tests and other obscene "measures of accountability" day and night, there have been a few moments when I looked at the brochures my friends the ex-teachers/now-in-real-estate passed me. Still, this is who I am, and I'm pretty settled into it.

Y'see, I'm a quiet teacher, not the kind with lots of performance flare and a ready joke to keep the classes entertained, but still, the kind that makes a difference one-on-one with some of the kids that everybody else misses or gives up on. I say things like, "You have a good answer here, you just gotta say more, say what YOU think." I'm good on building their strengths. I do a lot of thinking too, planning, on how to reach the ones that need some turning around, some fork in the road to get someplace different from nowhere. I even spend a lot of time worrying about crazy things like values. I mean, I don't think we've done our job if all they want is to buy an expensive pair of jeans with someone else's name on their butt. Then, some teacher with fake blue eyes in the next classroom comes in, batting her eyelashes at me and complaining that if only teacher salaries weren't so low, she could buy one of those fantastic (but ugly, she admits) purses that costs twenty times what her cute discount-store one does. I just mumble back to her my favorite Mexican saying, "*Solo lo barato se compra con dinero*" which means something along the lines of "Only cheap stuff can be bought with money." She just looks at me weird and reminds me she doesn't speak Spanish anymore, she forgot it all when she started first grade.

So, I keep looking for someone else who sees all this craziness, someone who might be able to do something about it, open people's eyes, educate us or something. But as *tímido* as I am, and as few conversations as I ever start with anybody, even if I found him, what would I say to him?? I'd probably just bump into him, mumble something like "Excuse me," stare at my shoes, and keep on walking. Only a pushy *duende*-type imaginary THING like I'd been caught by could possibly even keep a conversation going with me.

IT forced me up early on Saturday morning to pick the pecans scattered among the brown leaves on my front yard. "*Fuera desperdicio,*" IT scolded me, "You wanna WASTE one of these?! *¡No tienes respeto!* No respect at all!"

"For you?"

"No, for THEM!" He was pointing at the pecans. "You know it was just about a month or two ago, the way I look at it, that these elders of yours . . ."

"The Pecans?"

He looked at me crossly as if I were a small child interrupting a formal speech.

". . . these elders of yours came to the rescue. Two young Coahuiltecan Indians, Yantli and Huilta, who'd decided to settle in the bend of the river in this then-unpopulated place, had just hit their first blistery "Norther" in San Antonio (or Yanaguana, as it was called a mere five centuries ago.) They were out of food, were aching from the cold, and couldn't stop coughing. By the early dark hours of the morning, the grinding bite of long-term hunger had them weak and they were beginning to not feel their toes. They were wondering if they'd be alive to see another sunrise. . . . It was SO cold that night that the earth itself seemed to shiver. The air they breathed cut into their lungs, and the skin on their knuckles scraped off every time they brushed against a tree or against the frigid, unyielding ground. Even the blood on their scrapes seemed hesitant to come out in this cold, but instead just painted small, red smudges on the strange, dry whiteness of their frozen hands.

"Then the winds came out suddenly, as winds do around here, and surely, the little food that would have been there to hunt was hiding someplace warm. . . . Their hearts dragged, and they avoided each others' eyes, not wanting the other to see how close each was to yielding to defeat, giving up the spirit, and simply ceasing to care.

"Then, the trees, your elders, spoke. They whispered, they groaned, they shouted. And by the next dawn, hundreds of fat round pecans began to fall to the ground. Raining down on Yantli and Huilta, slapping their heads, scolding their feet, calling them. They gathered pecans till they couldn't gather anymore. They ate their fill, and ate the next day as well, and the next week, and the next, and the next, and when the last of their store of pecans was being rationed out a handful per meal, the first of spring's flowers began to bloom, and berries and young prey began to appear. They never forgot the gift from their elders, the trees."

"So that's how they kept the first San Antonians alive?"

"You ain't heard nothing yet! A few weeks ago . . . okay, like maybe seven, eight decades, the people were struggling again. Modern factories had arrived, but all it had done was increase the distance between what was considered wealthy, and what was considered poor. And the poor were working so many hours in dark, pecan-dust-filled factories, shelling pecans, that their fingers bled and the coughs raked over their lungs like steel claws. All so some candy company owner could get rich and throw away more. They even threw away people! TB was rampant, and the owners didn't even blink when workers had to be carried out. The *nueceros*, Mexican pecan shellers, most of them women, were dying to feed their children, and dying when they worked the hours it took to stay at the nicer end of starving. But they were still starving. Wages were so low, starvation so high that when a flu or cold season would come, entire families were carried out of their shacks in body bags. Even the authorities couldn't figure out how the pecan shellers survived on what they made. But it was the pecans, the pecans themselves that kept them alive. The protein in the nuts was often all they got.

"Then, the factories decided they needed more profits, and cut the wages in half. Hunger made the workers' choices clear. There was no risk greater than the one they already faced. They decided to strike, and they chose a leader …the young woman with her fist held high, and her voice held higher, made them dream again….made them believe something was possible. They lived on soup lines made from nothing, fed their families on air and faith and a few pecans that fell from the trees.

"They won the strike. Despite all that came after that, it was enough to plant hope. And to keep us alive."

Its voice had dropped to such a shivery whisper that I hardly noticed IT had stopped speaking. By now, we had both slumped into the open front seat of my junky, colorless car in the driveway.

I ran my fingers over the smooth surface of the pecan, trusting it like it was a bead in a rosary prayer. The crowds of teens that flocked to the weekend arts festival at the little park down the street had begun to arrive, shuffling into loosely assembled crowds at the corner traffic lights, waiting to cross. I stared at them, at their smooth brownness, almost the same shade as that of the pecan in my hand.

"*¿Entiendes?*" IT asked.
"Yeah," I breathed out slowly, like rising from a deep sleep," If it wasn't for THEM, the pecans, you wouldn't be alive."

"You got it wrong, guy. I'm a dream. I'm always alive, with or without you. If it wasn't for them, YOU wouldn't be alive."

It hit me like a slap, and I blamed it on the look in his eyes, the cold awareness he brought to my own sense of being. I could feel my soul disappearing, my parents' names being erased from history, my limbs beginning to vanish into the crisp air.

I stared at the pecan in my hand again, as if it were my grandfather. It took a few minutes before I could even speak. Then, just as I started to open my mouth, IT interrupted. Again.

"Okay, so let's get to work. First thing we need is. . . . Hmmm, *a ver* . . . sometimes everything hinges on one person. A leader. A real one. Forget Big Names, popularity, wealth . . . too weak. . . . We need. . . . That One! Over there, in that crowd."

"The guy with the broad shoulders, smiling?"

"No, the girl with a backpack on her shoulder, the little short one."

IT pointed toward a crowd of young people that was beginning to gather at the far corner of my block.

"But she's just a kid . . . maybe seventeen, eighteen years old! I'd probably get arrested for child molestation if I went up and asked her to come . . . listen to my dreams."

"She's the one we need," IT smiled.

"What makes you so sure?"

"Go ask her what her name is. Ask her where she's from. What she's doing in San Antonio. Go!"

Why I was listening to this insane figment of my imagination I don't know, but I ran like a madman down to the street corner and pushed my way to the center of the crowd waiting at the traffic light.

Mustering absolutely every crumb of eloquence I've ever had in my life, I turned to the girl and said, "Hi." Wincing from the pain that being so bold always caused me, I instinctively turned my gaze away, but surprisingly she answered, "Hello."

"Um. Big crowd for the *Feria de Artes* today, huh?"

She smiled and nodded, glanced back at the traffic light. Her large golden brown eyes danced like agate marbles when she smiled, but other than that, she was just another cinnamon-brown Chicana college kid in the crowd, and plain as worn blue jeans on a street full of

San Antonio teenagers. The traffic light turned, and she crossed with the crowd. My timidity fell back into place like a swig of hard liquor down an alcoholic's throat. I'd failed. Whatever it was IT wanted me to do, I hadn't done it. I didn't even understand why it was so important. My shuffling steps dreaded returning to my car, but I did.

"Well?" IT asked.

"Um. I guess we need to try something different."

"Correction. *You* need to try something different. I'm headed off. I wanna go check out the pecan pralines they're selling at that *tiendita* a few blocks over," IT said, reaching for the car door handle.

"Aren't you going to help me??" I must have shouted at a volume higher than polite, street conversation.

"I already did. Now you can finish it up."

"What do you mean?? I'm lost. I don't even know what I'm searching to accomplish!"

"You'll figure it out. Go find her again. Help her. *She's* the one with the important work to do."

"I don't get it! I don't get it! I don't even know why I should CARE."

"Just follow, *vato*. Just follow. It's not what's at the *end* of the road. It's the *road*. It's *traveling* the road. See you later, alligator!" he said, then dove through the trees in my neighbors' yard and disappeared.

I realized I was trembling, but for the life of me, I couldn't figure out why. I figured I was scared I'd never see him again. But I knew I was also horrified at the thought that he might never leave me.

I hunted her down again, followed her madly through the crowd. Walked right up, as awkwardly as probably I'd ever done anything in my life, tapped her on the shoulder and asked, "Um, uh- excuse me. I, uh, um – uh. What's your name?"

"Alma," she answered, with a bemused half-smile, "Alma de la Fuente. Why?"

"Are you from here?"

"No, I come from a tiny little town you've probably never heard of. Couple hours south of here. Alma Seca."

"Alma Seca? Isn't that the town where the Virgin of Guadalupe appeared on a Holy Tortilla about sixteen, seventeen years ago?"

"Yup, same town."

"Wow. Did you ever meet the family it happened to?"

"I GUESS you could say I met them. Mom. Dad. My sister, brothers. . . ."

"That was YOUR home?"

She nodded.

"You SAW the Holy Tortilla?"

"SAW it? I nibbled on it when no one was looking! Well, on the *masa*, anyway. Tasted pretty good, as I remember."

————◦◦◦————

And so began a long and weird friendship, a three-way friendship, between me, and her, and IT. She goes to college. I tutor her in Freshman Comp once a week, and then, when she leaves, I take notes. Take notes and learn. Learn, and wait. And IT mumbles over my shoulder, haranguing, critiquing, laughing, throwing pecans at my hunched back.

So that's why I'm here at home, grinding *comino* seeds in my *molcajete* before I get to that long list of things I know I gotta do. Grinding slowly, remembering what she told me about her dreams, remembering and trying to do all I can to clear the path. For what, I don't know, but getting ready for it anyway. I get scared too. The thought of getting others to recognize *familia, conección*, full circles, the quietness of still waters. . . .

Sometimes I wonder how my life got this way. I mean, it's not like a boss asked me to do it, or anything – it's me – just me that decided it has to be done - and done NOW. I did it, didn't I? Something inside me? Or maybe, something that didn't used to be inside me, but I was walking between the trees – those old, big, unpretentious ones out by Brackenridge Park, and it grabbed me. And now, it's just too late. If I rip it out of my heart, I'll bleed too much, and I won't survive – not the me that is me, not the me that has grown into and around and part of . . . this dream, centuries old, that comes from right here, right here . . . between the trees in the park, where I tend to spend a lot of time now.

Here. Care for a pecan? Delicious, right? Enjoy. Wondering why you feel strange? Well, it has something to do with the dirt, comes up the trunks of the trees into the pecans, through the plant roots into the *comino*, into the tacos, up through the stalks into the corn kernels, the corn tortillas, then it moves from visions of a Virgin into the dreams of the people, into *your* dreams. There is only a coolness to the air, the edge of excitement, an emotion that leaves its shadow there. Yeah, it's yours now, too. Don't be surprised. Dreams love to share. But they never like to die.

Black Leather Lu

I don't know her name. In fact, I don't even know if she's a she. But I look for her every morning, when I drive down Hildebrand St. on the way to work, and every afternoon, whether on the way home or to visit my daughter.

I worry about her. Why is she always there, even when I pass at different hours? Where does she sleep? I've seen her maybe ten times now, always on Hildebrand. Does she live nearby? When I don't see her, I look for her.

—◆—

It's been a rough month. My boss announced today that down-sizing would mean some major changes. Then, he raised his eyebrows in a particularly ungraceful way, and that must have been the period at the end of his sentence, 'cause he turned and left the room. Judy looked over at me, and I at her, and Paul didn't look at anybody. Hector just looked at his feet, like he always does when the boss talks. For a moment, no one breathed. Then, a sigh kinda started at one end of the room and moved through to the other, like when it takes a moment to catch your breath after a scary movie and the credits are running. So the sigh passed through us, and then we all just raised our eyebrows too, hopefully more gracefully than he had.

That was just the beginning of it, cause then the TV news started talking about higher gas prices and federal budget cuts to both food stamp programs for the poor and healthcare programs for the elderly. Ouch. That hits me at both ends, cause my 80-year-old Dad takes like 10 medicines a day, and my 20-year-old daughter's been on food stamps since the seventh month of her pregnancy when the doctor made her quit work. If they're pinched, I'm pinched.

I don't like to worry, but I figure my chances are 1 in 3 of being laid off. Paul is the boss's favorite, so that leaves me, Judy, and Hector. Rather than sweat and hyperventilate, I start to make a list in my head of what I have to fall back on if things get tough. I'm not doing too good with the list. Yeah, so I finally make this big decision to part with that box of really cool clothes from 10 years ago – so what? Once the decision to sell'em at garage sale is made, you realize they don't exactly look as cool now as they once did, and they probably won't bring in enough money to pay for the poster board for garage sale signs. The hideaway pockets in old purses had already been raided months ago, when my daughter had the baby, and I've already cut my cable bill down so much that most nights, I have a choice of news, cartoons, or some big TV evangelist that says I should turn everything over to Jesus, and here's the phone number in case I need to send in some money to their program.

Sometimes, nothing works as well as escape. So I grab the last of the banana pecan ice cream in the freezer and turn on the TV to the evangelist. Not too bad, especially after I turn off his volume and stick a CD in, pretending Reverend Pat is some kind of opera singer that sings soft rock.

<hr>

The first time I saw Black Leather Lu was different from the other times. I was about a block away, and I only saw her from behind. She was sauntering in a sassy, strong, long-legged way. She was wearing a fringed black leather jacket, tight black jeans, and high-heeled black leather boots, and the way she was sauntering looked like she was feeling on top of the world, aware of how good she looked and proud of it. Her short, blonde hair was perfectly combed, and a small cordovan-colored purse was slung over her shoulder. Confident, together, sexy – or so it seemed from behind. The day was sunny and crisp, nice breeze blowing, and I smiled, proud for her, and happy to see someone saunter to match the day.

The second time I saw her, the saunter didn't seem as happy. Then I passed her. And even from the glimpse in the rear view mirror, there was something about the heavily rouged cheeks and mascara'd eyes that looked a bit off-kilter. She was tall and strong and dressed stylishly, but the magic of the confident saunter, to the observer, was gone.

<hr>

I love my neighborhood. Hildebrand Street is one of those neat parts of the city where you can find a little bit of everything. It's not like those neighborhoods where there's gates around them and only people with the magic code can get in. This place is a lot more open. On one block, you've got these great big, old, plantation-type houses, and on the next, you've got these little bitty, miniature houses built on a skinny half-lot, their elaborate, tiny gardens spilling over with twenty different colors of flowers.

One of the elderly couples there always shows its support for the city basketball team during Play-offs by spelling "Go Spurs Go" in big letters made of white styrofoam cups squished into the diamond-shaped holes on their Allied fence. Then, there's the garage apartments that are really barely-redone garages, and the studio apartments that are just an empty studio. Some of the larger, older homes have owners that can't afford to fix them up, so they just break them into lots of crumbly, one-room apartments, and desperate college students live there, learning to co-exist with the cockroaches. Then, a block behind them is the elegant street where the university president lives, and the centuries-old tree that has its roots always pushing up the asphalt of the street and breaking it into chugholes – and nobody complains.

But you can't go five buildings in a row and not find something different: a coffee shop, an apartment complex, an estate with a big rock wall, an artist's collaborative with experimental purple paint on the front porch. And less than five minutes away by car or fifteen minutes by bus, a big community college, and a block more over, The Esperanza Peace and Justice Center, which most folks just call The Esperanza, cause that's what it gives – *esperanza*, hope, to everyone who needs it, even if you're what the neighborhoods consider "too different, too weird." At The Esperanza, they know we're *all* different, *all* weird. That's the neighborhood here, and most of the time, we get along pretty well, the university profs, the artists, the college kids, the unemployed, the construction workers we carry Cokes out to when they fix our streets, the slumlords, the activists, and the retired couples. It's a nice little pocket about a mile from downtown and maybe fifty blocks big, and most of us wouldn't want to live anywhere else. Then, at the top of the neighborhood, there's Hildebrand Street.

There's things here on Hildebrand you wouldn't find anywhere else in town, right along with all the essentials like the Magic Touch Body Shop and El Puffy Taco. A run-down, sometimes-in-business, second-hand/antique store always has a tiny Mexican flag planted undecorously in the front yard. Walk into "Roy's Appliance and Parts" and you'll think you stepped back into 1960, with John F. Kennedy's Presidential Photo proudly hung to your right, and in front of you – shelf after shelf of tiny boxes with lamp harps, replacement cords, and pressure cooker rings covering the entire wall from the floor to the ceiling. The man at the counter will pick up his magnifying glass to study the model number of any appliance you carry in, and within minutes, he's got you not only the part, but elaborate instructions on how to install it good as new. This in a time period when nobody will fix anything – just throw it in the trash and buy a new one at Wal-Mart. Now you see why I like my neighborhood?

It's busy and business on this block of Hildebrand, but the trash cans and the back doors of garages facing the street a block down from here remind you that this was once the quiet alley to the large and elegant houses of a wealthy residential district. It's still a quiet residential area if you walk half-a-block off Hildebrand. Then, the trees, the cats, and the run-down or fixed up, tiny or large, lavish or starving houses remind you that people live here. Real people, with real needs. The old soda-fountain drug store still delivers prescriptions out to elderly customers who can't safely drive their luxury 1971 Oldsmobile Delta 88's anymore, and the WIC Clinic still receives a line of single mothers and their infant children waiting to receive food coupons that will let them get free milk, free formula, and free bread. Somehow, the WIC mothers feel sorry for the affluent elderly, and the affluent elderly feel sorry for the WIC mothers. They pass on the street and make space for each other, smiling politely, and grateful too for the other's consideration.

———◆———

Lu's rouge is extreme today – doesn't look good. Big red streaked squares seem to torture each of her cheeks, and her lipstick is smeared and off the lips, almost as if some giant clumsy hand from the sky had tried to paint it on a miniature doll. Is she not feeling well? Is she mentally ill? There's a desperate look in her eyes today, or at least from as much as I can tell in the rear-view mirror. Her clothing is not as stylishly arranged as usual, as if she'd pulled herself together quickly and not all the parts were there.

When I mention Black Leather Lu to my street-savvy daughter, she corrects me flatly, "Mom. It's a guy!" "No," I insist, "The black-leathered one I saw was a girl. Yes, tall, kind of broad-shouldered, cordovan purse. But it's a girl. She had a low-cut blouse and–"

"Mom. It's a guy."

"But . . ." She's already shaking her head as only children can at their parents' innocence.

"Yeah, he's crazy. He always hangs out on Hildebrand and acts crazy and cusses out the cars. He carries a purse, and puts on his makeup, and always wears black leather. Mom, it's a guy."

I keep calling her "Lu." I figure, whether Lu or Lou, either way it works.

—◦—

The next time I see her, she's really in bad shape. She's at the corner of Hildebrand and Blanco, gesturing at every car that passes and looking really angry. They lock their car doors and look away. Nobody cusses her back. She forgot to put her blouse on, but the fringed jacket still falls carefully over the breasts, revealing only the tired, floppy cleavage.

—◦—

Radio news keep blaring at me, "No Child Left Behind." What in the world does that mean? That we all have to go exactly the same pace, same place, same drummer, and only on command? . . . I been reading this really weird book. It's about a guy who shows up for an ad asking for someone who wants lessons on how to save the world. Turns out the teacher is a gorilla, named Ishmael, reads a lot, teaches the guy a lot. How modern humans have tried to wipe out all other forms of life, and take control. How nature likes diversity cause it helps survival, but "Taker cultures" want things uniform. Makes control easier, so they eliminate diversity, set the planet on a death-course.

Anyway, the gorilla gets sold to a circus, and eventually the damp, cold weather does the gorilla in. And the guy is left to wonder about all the things the gorilla didn't finish teaching him.

For some reason, it makes me think of the hospital, when my daughter went in to have the baby. She knew all the things the birthing class teaches you. Don't lie flat on your back, walk – it's less painful. The more pain medication you have, the slower the dilation goes, and the more they wanna break your water to make things speed up. Once they break your water, you're on a time clock with only 24 hours (or a lot less) to dilate bfore they insist on a C-section. One out of every four births now is a C-section. She'd heard all that stuff, and she'd even written about her preferences: who she wanted in the birthing room, what forms of pain relief she perferred, no IV's so she could walk around freely and let labor progress faster, bring the baby to her right after birth, etc. . . .

But somehow, once you get in there, a giant medical machine takes over, and you are passed along an assembly line that knows how THEY want things done, and YOU are just a prop, a small screw on an assembly belt, which they will adjust and insert as they need it.

Within an hour, they had her strapped down flat on the bed, IV's sticking in her on both sides, and an anesthesiologist telling her that an epidural was the only sure way to handle the pain. Then the doctor broke her water, and within two hours of that, the nurses AND the doctor were shaking their heads and saying, "A C-section is the only safe way to go, for your baby's health."

A whole C-section, lots of lost blood, and a healthy baby later, she was looking up at me in a daze, saying, "Where's my baby? Why don't they bring me my baby?" Don't get the idea we didn't put up a fight, but sometimes those BIG machines just plow forward and nobody better get in their way or they'll get steamrolled over. That's what the hospital felt like. And more so when they saw she was on food stamps; it's like she was suddenly a bad mom and a stupid one, too. They brought her the baby when they wanted, and took it away when they wanted, too.

"She needs to drink two ounces every two hours" the nurse said snippily, and woke the baby from a deep slumber to force her onto the breast. "If she doesn't get enough from you, we'll give her the two ounces of formula back in the nursery so she doesn't dehydrate.

But then, she may not be hungry to beastfeed after that." Talk about pressure when you're fumbling to learn a new and not so automatic skill with a chewed, sore nipple and a large, unhealed incision on your tummy. After a couple dozen tries or more, the baby finally got the hang of it and latched on, glugging the clear, natural liquid down eagerly, and my daughter breathed a sigh of relief. But within five minutes, the nurse appeared again, "Ready for your nap, little one?" and whisked away the still-hungry, wide-awake baby back to the nursery, where two hours later, they would jolt her awake again. Soon, both mother and baby were tired, hungry, and irritable, jolted from their own sleep cycles to fit some recommended schedule. And this Giant Machine just kept rolling forward, threatening to crush anyone in its perfectly scheduled path.

I started watching the clock, counting the hours till I could get them out of there, to a place where they could sleep when they're sleepy and eat when they're hungry. This institution, it seems, is not into diversity. But they ARE a LOT into control. My daughter survived the experience, but only, I'm convinced, because we got her out of there on the third day, right before they wore her down totally.

<hr />

We get the word from the boss. It's Judy that's gonna go. She isn't fazed. That girl has *gracia*. She just flicks her long, thick, grey and white braid to the back, and announces that she used to make twice this much money as a waitress, she can always go back. She's unruffled and convincing, but the limp in her feet as she moves to the coat rack makes Hector and me exchange a cautious glance. She's trim and muscular, petite, active, and in great shape for 52. But everyone including the boss remembers her complaining about how much her feet have been hurting lately. God, we're gonna miss her. Especially on those exhausting days when the work gets tedious and the tasks get huge; her large, sparkly black eyes always have a smile in them, as she cracks jokes and keeps us all on task. Hector looks like he's gonna cry. Judy puts a hand on his shoulder and transmits strength, just like she always does. The boss leaves as soon as he's told us, adding that further cuts might "reduce hours, but employees who work hard will have the least reductions." Chicken-shit coward doesn't even stay around to say goodbye to her, but Paul does, taking a superior fatherly role, funny for someone 29, and shakes her hand, something he's never done before. Paul works less than anyone except the boss, but the boss likes him because– well, I guess because he's the one that most reminds him of himself. I guess Judy's the one who reminds him least of himself. Female. Hard-working. Smart. Honest. Unafraid of anything. Dark as chocolate. Mexican-American.

The boss has those eyes that are called blue, but if you look at 'em carefully they're just the lack of color, like clear water pooled on a sidewalk. Paul's eyes are green, but he's the only one of the rest of us that has light skin. I find that I've been staring at the creamy tan color of the skin on my hands, lost in my thoughts, wondering what subconscious color images made the boss "like" me more than Judy, or whether it was the fact that she's unafraid of anything, unlike me, who still cringes a lot at stories in the news.

For the first time, I see Black Leather Lu actually soliciting someone. She is pink and pale, and the makeup is funny again. A guy sits in a car in the parking lot of the car wash. The guy looks like he's waiting for someone. Lu, leopard-print purse slung over her shoulder, approaches him. The guy shakes his head but doesn't seem bent outta shape. Some folks woulda gotten more scared by Lu, but he just shakes his head and waves bye and goes back to adjusting the dials on his radio. Was Lu just asking him for a cigarette, or scoping him out? Lu walks on; the saunter seems unsteady. The heels today seem wobbly, the head not quite straight.

Radio news on the way home: Higher Budget Needed for War. Dismantling Social Security because it's too expensive. And Privatizing. From what I can figure, this last thing means it's their private business to give you anything if they want to, and if they don't, it's your private business to deal with whether you starve. You gotta watch it with listening to the news – it can drive you crazy. It's hard to stay sane listening to the new versions of what's true. Hector's worried that if his income taxes go any higher, or his income goes any lower, they won't be able to even buy the girls uniforms for school. They make good use of garage sales for everything else they need, but uniforms? Used uniforms don't last the first two minutes at garage sales.

I offer to keep an eye out for uniforms at the garage sales. Hector's really grateful. I only found two little blouses this last summer, and they tried to pay me for them, but I refused. His wife sent me four dozen homemade tamales at Christmas, and I felt guilty that I'd gotten the WAY better end of the deal.

He's sitting on the curb by the corner bus stop, smoking a cigarette and banging a newspaper angrily on his black-leathered knee. His whisps of blonde hair are waving in time to the paper-banging. Occasionally, the sneering mumble of some articulated comment distorts his lips, as he seems to talk to someone not visible to our eyes. Today, he is not well. The city has announced new rules cracking down on the homeless. I wonder, where do they expect them to go? Home?

I wonder also if the new ordinance will apply to people who dress strangely and spend a lot of time on the street. I can just see the police coming to get Lu, to protect the city's "image" of having no homeless and no weird people. Maybe those folks at City Hall trying to protect our "image" don't really know who we, the city, are.

Summary of the TV News tonight: we have freed the people of Iraq after killing about a thousand of them in the war we declared. Then we helped them have an election, so they can have a government just like ours. Now they will be free to have McDonald's and C-sections and be a civilized country, just like us. I wonder if there's any ice cream left in the freezer. I think my Dad finished it yesterday – damn the diabetes torpedoes, full speed ahead!

Lu is paler, pinker than usual. He's wearing classic high-heeled pumps, and a beautiful black hat. He is trying to float gracefully down the street. A small brown dog is following him safely, at a distance, also trying.

‹‹———››

Hector's eyes were red at work today - he's been asking me if I know anybody that can help him get rid of his accent. He was born in Mexico, he confesses, came over as a teenager, but never lost the accent. He's taking night classes to improve his English, maybe get some college credit? I tell him I think his English is fine – it sounds very pleasant and very San Antonio, gives him a nice image. He smiles hopefully, but seems nervous still. Doesn't hang around after work like he used to when Judy would joke and lay out cups of coffee on the front table to congratulate us on a "Good day's work, Team!" He grabs the lunchbox his wife packs him and runs out to catch the bus that'll get him to the community college before class starts. His wife'll pick him up after his class, when she's cleaned two houses, picked up the girls from school, made supper, and bathed the girls. He'll eat supper, do the minor repairs on the three apartments in the old frame house that convince the owner to keep his rent low, and study his English again, trying to wipe out any trace of "foreignness" that might make the boss think he's not "working hard enough."

I'm having a hard time keeping myself from going crazy. I wonder how hard it must be for Lu to keep from going crazy. Nobody tells me what I should dress like, who I should be – or who I should think I am. At least not recently.

The ten o'clock news has a story about illegal immigration. No one mentions how the guys on the Mayflower also crossed into this country with no permission. I make a note to tell Hector about what my Gramma used to say. She was this really neat lady who always drilled me on saying my WHOLE name, Mexico-style, even though she was born here, and her family had lived here since before it was Texas or Mexico or even New Spain. And she also taught me HER whole name – Diamante Daniela Ibarra Salazar de Huizar. She always used to say I was *perlada*, like her father, who'd been a well-respected fighter for justice. Said "Don't let them tell you all Mexicans are brown. All *human beings* are brown! Some of us are chocolate and some of us are *café con leche*, some are vanilla milk and some are deep black-brown coffee. And we ALL have a right to be here!" That's what she always said. Then she'd shake her head and add, "Tell that Statue of Liberty lady to look for us too, look this way, light that torch for those who come from the same continent!" Yeah, Hector would have liked her. Judy woulda liked her even more.

My car breaks down on the way to work, but a friendly forty-ish guy standing at the bus stop on Hildebrand and San Pedro pops open the hood, sticks in a screwdriver, and diagnoses it as "too rich a mixture" or something. I need to have the timing fixed. Driving home, I realize I haven't seen Lu for three days – I worry, is he okay?

Best part of the weekend – a garage sale. Friday, during lunch, I go to pay my light bill in person and I pass a garage sale right on my way, so I stop. I LOVE garage sales! On any good Saturday, you can find fifteen one-of-a-kinds in an hour – items, styles, colors that two dozen stores at the mall won't have. Most stores only stock the latest four styles, in the latest five colors, or if you're lucky, the latest FIVE styles (in only four colors.) You could spend weeks and not find the color you're looking for. They don't "make" it this year. Try looking for MY favorite color, teal. No way – this year's blues are indigo & dusty heather. But right here, at my first garage sale, I find a deep-teal velvet blouse, with the tag still on it. Someone must've gotten it as a Christmas present, wrong size, and finally given up trying to fit into it. . . . Their loss, my gain – seventy-five cents! . . . I love garage sales – I tell you. They're better 'n ice cream.

Finally, on Saturday, driving my car to my cousin's to see if he can fix it, I see Lu again. He's angry. Standing menacingly at the bus stop, ready to insult the bus, banging a compact umbrella against his leg as if it were a steel macana. He isn't smiling at anyone. Most of his angry gestures are at a spot halfway into the street, where no one's standing. There's no blouse, no purse, just the black fringed jacket, jeans, boots, and makeup. I can't figure out what he's saying. The light changes and I try to read his lips in the rear view mirror. Maybe he's braver than all of us. Maybe he's smarter too.

Monday (seems to always be our lucky day at work, huh?) Boss announces he'll be paying the errands by the job insteada by the hour. . . . Hector does about 4 a day in addition to the office work. Now, he'll clock in and out for the office work, and be paid only $4.90 per errand. . . . I ask him, how many errands do you usually run in a day? 4. How many will you have to run to get the same pay now? 6. Will you finish in time for class at the community college? He doesn't answer.

Judy's sick. Hector told me. Said his wife dropped by to leave her some *arroz con pollo* this weekend, and found her in bed, unable to walk. It's one of those strange diseases where the muscles quit working one section of the body at a time. She doesn't really have any family that she still speaks to. We start an envelope at the office. Paul says he'll send a check with a personal note from home. We know he won't.

Hector's always got rings under his eyes these days, and today I even thought I heard him pronouncing his last name with an English accent. . . . ROD-rug-ezz. His wife only got paid for one house today, because she got a call from the school that her daughter wasn't in appropriate uniform. So who thought anyone would notice if a 7-year-old had a flat-front khaki skirt instead of a pleated one? By the time she got her changed and back to school, it was already time to get to the second house, so she missed half of what she would've been paid that day. Hector admitted to me that he'd even be tempted to go home to Mexico, except that the Mexico he was born in doesn't exist anymore. Then he shrugs his shoulders and asks if I think he should start looking for another job?

———✦———

Today I see Lu happy and sauntering, and I slow the car down. Is it the sunshine? Is it a delusion? I've started marking down the dates I see her on the flattened paper bag in the CD compartment.

In February, I have the car wreck. The car is totaled. The pain in my neck keeps me from being able to do the paperwork at the office. Scared the boss'll let me go. My Dad's Social Security check wouldn't even be enough to pay the utilities. Somehow can't part with the car, even though I know it's totaled, so I just have them tow it to the back yard and leave it there. This way, even though I'm taking the bus, I don't feel car-less.

I heard from Judy's friend, the waiter, today. The doctors are talking about putting a tube into her throat so she can eat. It's hard to understand her words these days – her friend the waiter translates. This thing she has affects everything. It starts with the feet and the legs, then the arms, then the tongue. Eventually, the throat forgets how to swallow, and the heart forgets how to beat.

I make it to work almost every day, but the last two hours are hell. When I get home, I lay down. I haven't even been over to see my daughter and baby granddaughter. Hector's wife somehow manages to squeeze in a visit every other weekend and brings me some *caldo* or tacos. Now she's got two of us – me and Judy – to watch over. That woman's amazing. I don't know how she does it.

It's been two months since the wreck and I'm still dragging myself to therapy three times a week, right after work. When will I get better? My Dad's got a cough that won't go away, and I haven't had a chance to go to the drugstore to get his prescription filled. I haven't even had a chance to prick his finger to check blood sugar like I'm supposed to do every day. Maybe on the weekend.

But by the weekend, I just lie in bed all day long, too sick to get up, I think my blood pressure's up, but I don't have the energy to go to the drugstore and check it on the machine they have there. My Dad calls Hector's wife – when did she give him her number? She comes over and sits her girls in front of my TV, cleans my house, and cooks a wonderful *arroz con pollo* supper. I sleep till Monday. . . .

On the bus to work Monday, I peer out the window and realize suddenly I haven't seen Lu in a very long time. I fear something's happened to him. An inexplicable stream of guilt goes through me at my neglect or forgetting, or my something, I'm not sure what.

At the office, a lady comes in with three little ones, trying to juggle her checkbook, billpaying, and childcare. The tiny one's asleep in her arms, the diapered toddler is screaming his head off, and the oldest, who appears to be a young four or so, is quietly studying the posters on our walls. In an effort to head off any further problems for the lady, I pull out one of the coloring pages the City Water Board gives away, that have pictures of a lawn with orange trees.

I guide her to a table and chair where she can hopefully write her check and juggle the younger two, as I chirp to the well-behaved four-year-old, "Would you like to color?"

The little girl nods. I hand her the coloring page and head back for the small jar of crayons we keep under the counter, handing her the first one that comes out of the jar. It's purple, and I realize my mistake as I see the large simple drawing of outlined oranges on an outlined green tree on an outlined green lawn. "Here," I say, magnanimously handing her an orange crayon.

"Why do the oranges have to be orange?" she asks pointedly, eyeing the myriad of other colors in the jar. Stunned, I leave the entire glass jar on her table, ignoring the boss's warning never to do so.

The lady manages to get the check signed and the toddler quieted, but I keep my eye on the 4-yr-old, still stunned. "Wait!" I shout, rather awkwardly, as the lady starts to go out the door. I fumble in my purse, and hand the little girl a full pack of gum. She thanks me, and they are soon back in the parking lot, maneuvering the sleeping baby back into a carseat and the toddler into another, while the four-year-old crawls into a booster seat and buckles herself. I stare at her all the way out of the parking lot, till all I can see of her still is the very top of a little, brown pony tail. The glass jar of crayons is catching the sunlight on the table as if it were a centerpiece, and I sense something deep inside me fall back into place, as if the broken, misplaced pieces of a puzzle had suddenly healed themselves.

The next weekend is different. I'm up early, on the bus, and over to my cousin's house, who says simply, "You shoulda called me earlier! *Todo tiene remedio.*" I wonder if he's being tutored by the little girl with the ponytail. Within two weeks, he's doctored my car back into life – green fender, blue bumper, silver door, but every part there.

"You're gonna get stares. You sure you don't mind?" he probes in his off-handed way.

"Hey," I laugh, stealing my Dad's line, "It's a car, not a shirt. It's to drive me places, not to wear on my body."

Still, when the day comes for me to pick it up from him, he's borrowed a buddy's can of body paint, and I'm looking at an all-grey, not-perfect paint job on a car that runs reliably without stopping and with no parts falling off.

I feel invincible. On Monday morning, I'm in my deep-teal velvet blouse, dangling earrings, and my hair all set and sexy. I'm gonna make it. The world is gonna make it. Dad is even gonna make it.

Driving down Hildebrand, suddenly, I see Black Leather Lu. She's walking facing me, on the same side of the street. I look at her eyes, checking for that bad-shape look she'd had last time, but she is feeling good. She doesn't have the saunter down, and the makeup isn't as convincing as her early days, but she gives me a big smile and a thumbs-up, "Right-On" gesture as I pass. I don't know if it's because of the newly painted color of my car, or because she approves of my hair and makeup, but it's a clear affirmation anyway. I laugh. Here I am, getting my hair and makeup approval from someone who frequently streaks uneven red squares of rouge on her cheeks, but I feel good anyway. Yup, even Black Leather Lu is gonna make it.

⟶⟵

Judy died last week. She had asked for a no-trouble, no-non-sense, no-service cremation, but Hector, his wife, the waiter who was taking care of her, and I decided to have a memorial service anyway, with a few friends and some coffee and tacos, of course.

Hector's English is better, but he still sweats and looks at his feet whenever the boss walks in. I've started doing the rehab exercises at home too, and my neck is really improving. I can usually make it all the way to 5 o'clock without hurting, and I sometimes give Hector a ride to community college so he doesn't have to take the bus. Some weekends I even babysit their two girls alongside my granddaughter. I hit almost every garage sale I see, as long as I've got more than 75 cents in my purse, and I drive down Hildebrand proudly in my green-blue-silver car painted grey. Sometimes I even find a cool garage sale workshirt for my cousin. I read the news, but I don't take them seri-ously – I watch'm like watching a *telenovela*, remembering they're all fiction. I think about how the world should be, not how some people try to make it. Sometimes I see people getting bent outta shape, feel-ing like I did three months ago, with the world spiraling crazier and crazier around me. They read the newspaper, watch the news. Sweat.

I just send them thoughts that say, Don't let them lie to you. God is not on our side. He can't even stomach what we're doing. He's not on their side either. Whenever someone starts to claim God's "side", it's always a lie. God don't have sides. He's against all this mess. He doesn't like to scrap. He'd rather saunter down the street, feeling good, in a neighborhood that has both sides, and a bunch of others, living in it, without complaining.

Yes, God, with funny makeup and unclear gender, and not all the pieces there, hard to define, making people uncomfortable, looking sometimes good and sometimes unsettling, making us try hard to be non-judgmental, and making us remember that we are all created absolutely uniquely, but still totally, in His, or Her, image.

Tía

When she was 82, she lost her eyesight. Cataracts. Same year, she lost her husband. Two years later, the cholesterol and blood sugar were responsible for a severe loss of hearing. The niece that took care of her was the one that everyone turned to when someone got sick. Nice lady. Let her move in and cooked for her, *con mucho cariño.* Husband said, "Oh, well. It's just like when we had our babies. I don't mind."

By 89, she was having some serious problems with the diabetes. In 2 years, she lost two legs. "It's OK" said the niece, "I'll take care of her. She doesn't need to walk." But then the different parts of her started falling off. By 96, the whole day was bathing, giving medicine, changing diapers, and listening to groans. The night was worse. The husband left. The niece was now taking care of her aunt, an older sister, and her father. The aunt began to cough and some internist said she should be in the hospital. So they put her in. The niece came by every evening. Covered her with a bathrobe that only had to cover a shape two and a half feet long. The doctor said it wouldn't be long.

But after two months, the doctor had been transferred to a different hospital, and one of his eager and eminent replacements had dropped dead of a heart attack.

In the third month, the hospital social worker recommended she be moved to the "extended care" unit. The niece still came every evening, sitting by her side, holding the space that used to be her hand, and finally checking her watch and going home with a sigh, to prepare for her father's doctor visits the next day. "I feel like running away from home," she said. "But there's no one to take care of everyone. Nobody who'll do it. They'd all come hunt me down, to do the family chores. Sometimes, this sitting by Tía's side is the only quiet time I have."

The hospital social worker was re-assigned to a different unit, faces came and faces went. When they had to weigh her, they used the baby scales. She was under 40 pounds. "She can't last much longer," said the young doctor, new to the beat and soon to be gone.

She didn't speak anymore, but she coughed and she groaned, and the night nurse said to the niece, "Prepare yourself, honey: she doesn't have long. But she's going to a better place." After a while, the night nurse went on to a better position with a private foundation. Finally, Medicare said they couldn't cover any more hospital days that year. So her niece came with a lap blanket, wrapped her gently, and carried her home.

The niece was having chest pains regularly these days and her own children had all moved out of state. Her grandchildren were asking what was she going to leave them, what was the market value of her house, and did she have a DNR order? A Living Will?

The niece changed the diapers easier now that the aunt's weight had dropped even more. And the other sick family members had passed on and released her of her extra duties. The ex-husband never came by. And the brothers and sisters that had been too busy to take care of the aunt were still too busy to take care of the niece.

The niece lit a *vela* once every week, right after her trip to the grocery store, but soon she had made arrangements with a teenage neighbor to run the errands for her, for a small fee. Life got quieter, and the niece quit counting the years go by. Sometimes she felt that the only thing that got her up each morning was the knowledge that she had to change the diaper and prepare the corn *atole* – *atole* that she spoon-fed her tía – and occasionally tasted a spoonful of as well.

But finally the morning came when the clock had wound down, the spirit had run out, and the niece did not rise from her bed.

The house was quiet for a long time.

—◦—

"Well, it's old but I'm really happy with it. A good place for graduate work. You wouldn't believe this place! It's really, well . . . I dunno . . . like home. *Una casita chiquita, calladita*, but it's got something. . . .

"And there's a *Vela* to the Virgin of Guadalupe, at a little altar, and hand-crocheted doilies on the couch. Yeah, I got it with the furniture and everything. There's gobs of stuff here! The family didn't think a garage sale would be worth the trip down here, so they sold the whole thing at a flat rate and great terms, even let me move in right away and pro-rate the rent. . . . I can hardly wait to open up some of these trunks!"

She was right. The place was cozy. She noticed it changed her lifestyle right from the beginning. She started buying candles to the Virgin of Guadalupe and lighting them at the altar, and for some reason, she began cooking *atole*. There were so many pillows piled on the bed in the second bedroom, and several of them seemed to be antiques. She promised herself to get to that room as soon as she cleared away some of the stuff in the kitchen.

By the end of the first week, she was feeling the rhythm of the house, and at night she was dreaming, dreaming – of a flow like the ocean's tide - an in and out, a soothing repetitive pattern that sounded like life itself, like breathing. She quit working on the dissertation and began writing in her journal - writing between pots of *atole* or *sartenes* of *frijol con queso*. And sometimes a homemade *caldo* steeped all day till the nutrients filled the air, and she felt she could almost inhale their sustenance. The dreams of tides, of ins and outs, of the breath of life, began to fill her waking hours as well.

One night, she dreamed she was walking to the second bedroom and opening the trunk, peering inside and seeing things she recognized from long, long ago. She even picked it up - this thing she had never touched, but had somehow never forgotten. It was rounded and pulsing and smelled of corn being toasted, warmed, prepared Then she had approached the bed, and looked beyond the pillows till her own breathing had tied her to the universe. In the morning, she couldn't remember if she had really gone to that room, or merely dreamed of it.

The months passed. Her sense of peace deepened. There were three constants in life: the *atole*, the *vela* to the Virgin of Guadalupe, and the in-and-out of breathing that she heard more and more clearly each day, heard with something more than her ears, more than her heart, heard maybe with the life spirit that kept her going. She, or the house, or the air – or maybe someone else – was breathing.

By the time she met the niece's aunt, there was no surprise inside her. There was only the desire to cook *atole*, and the dedication to continue the breath of the ocean's life. If she could keep her alive, she could keep the universe alive. Tía was tiny by now, no more than an armful. And there was nothing left to lose, except her heartbeat and that obstinate soothing breath.

She fed her *atole*, or maybe the old woman inhaled it. All she knew was that the rhythms of her life had changed, and they followed the inhale and the exhale of the large cloudy brown eyes. When she was not cooking or buying *velas*, she wrote. And when she had ceased to light *velas*, the person who followed her read the writings.

These writings.

And they knew that if you listened very closely, you could hear her inhale, the universe, still alive. Do you hear it? Do you hear it now? Between the flickers of the *vela* in your living room. Between your footsteps as you walk to the kitchen, thinking of smooth, life-giving *atole* – thinking of sustenance so soft, so strong you can inhale it, in the particles of air, thinking of . . . life. . . .

Glossary

Spanish Terms and Phrases in order of appearance

Chencho's Cow

jugo – juice
papa con huevo – potato and egg
aguas frescas – lemonade-type drinks made from a variety of fruits
avena – oatmeal
¡Gringo entremetido! – Nosy Gringo!
la rica – Rich woman
masa – dough

La Santísima María Pilar

La Santísima – The Most Holy
¡Ay, y pónme a mí también! – Put it on me too!
fuchi – yucky
Me voy a ver bien cool. – I'm gonna look REAL cool.
cascarrones – confetti-filled, decorated egg shells
fajitas – barbecued strips of marinated skirt steak
anda cámbiale el pañal al bebé – go change the baby's diaper
esa es cosa de mujeres – that's women's stuff
aguacate – avocado
es su modo – that's the way he is
muy mandón – very bossy
calentar el orno – to warm up the oven
¿Que te pasa? – What's the matter?
¡Ay, Dios mío! – Oh, my God!
barbacoa de cabeza – a delicacy of ground-barbecued cow's head
un bebito – a baby
borracho – drunk
cuentos – stories
¡Qué mujer! – What a woman
baba – saliva

The Holy Tortilla

que rara – How odd
muy correcta – very proper
calmada – calm
molino – grinder
metate – traditional Mexican Indian grinding stone
masa – dough
novela – soap opera
amor inocente – innocent love
comal – iron griddle

desprecio – disdain
Sí, corazón. – Yes, dear heart.
paciencia – patience
pueblito – little town
limonada – lemonade
tunas – cactus fruit (from the prickly pear)
viejitos – old ones
con alma – with soul
No hay que llegar primero, pero hay que saber llegar. – You don't have to
    get there first, you just have to know how to get there
chanclas – Mexican sandles
y chulearles– and give loving attention to them
la migra – Slang for the Immigration Officers, the I.N.S.
devotos – devout folk
mojados – people who have crossed into the US without legal permission;
    translation of slang "wetbacks"
pachangas – large, festive gatherings
pa' quejarse tanto – to complain so much
primo – cousin
alma seca – dried-up soul
¡Que Gacho! – What a bummer!
Movimiento – Movement; refers to the Chicano Movement
regalos – gifts

The Pot has Eyes

jarro – clay pot
peltre – speckleware
¿Pero, que tiene eso que ver, Mamá? – But what does that have to do with it, Mama?
tú anda – go ahead
locuras – crazy things
ideas locas – crazy ideas
déjanos, por favor – leave us alone, please
nuca – nape of the neck
masa harina – pre-mixed flour for making tortillas
chiflado – spoiled
mi papá era indio – my father was an Indian

Inheritance

así suavecito – soft like that
y a'i vamos otra vez – and there we go again
ya ves – you see
a mano – by hand
la curaba – it would cure it, prepare it
como le pusieron – what did they call it
venía un indio – an Indian would come
¡Ay vienen los indios! – The Indians are coming!
y se enojaba – and she'd get mad

y allí mero pusieron su casa – and they put their house right there
cómo se llama – what's it called, "whatchamacallit"
o algo – or something
¿No te acuerdas? Ya 'staba built. – Don't you remember? It was already built.
juguetitos – little toys.
con esa sombra grandota – with that big old shadow
que quién sabe qué – and what all
¿Tan pocos? – So few?
rinconcito – little corner
pobrecitos – poor things
siglos – centuries
tatara–abuelo – great-great-grandfather
viz–abuelo – great-grandfather
lágrimas – tears
indio querido – beloved Indian
m'ija – my daughter, my child
chiquititita, así – so very small, like that
ahora sí me reconociste – now you finally recognized me
¿No ves, m'ijita? – Don't you see, my child?

Whispers from the dirt

¿Es todo? – That's all?
¿Dónde estará? – Where can she be?
¡No me abandonen! – Don't abandon me

Reclaiming

aquí – here
querido – beloved
bueno, no le hace – oh well, it doesn't matter

El Mojado No Existe (The Wetback Does Not Exist)

esos Steubens agarrados – those greedy Steubens
Simpático – nice
oficiante – official
chisme – gossip
¿Como siempre? – As always?
perlado – a pearl-colored complexion

Invisible

no seas mala – don't be mean

The Stuff to Scream With

muchacha – girl
bolillo – small roll of French bread
mocos – mucus
marranito – a gingerbread pig

y a'i viene una trocota – and there comes a big, old truck
ya va a comenzar La Escandalosa – the noisy one is going to start
to'o contentito – all happy
¡Cáyate, huerca! – Shut up, brat!
te doy un paletazo – I'll give you a beating
barbudo – unshaved

I Just Can't Bear It

abrazo – hug
pésame – condolences
¡Ay! ay! Que tristeza! – Oh, Oh. What sadness!
¡Se me quiebra el corazón! – my heart is breaking!
ay, no puedo . . . con este dolor – I can't bear this pain

Federico y Elfiria

no le hacía – it didn't matter
muy ranchera – very shy and unsophisticated
casa – home
muy galán – very "slick," rakishly handsome
a lo mejor – maybe
a las escondiditas – on the sly
de todos modos – anyway
trenza – braid
media llenita– kind of plump
flaca – skinny
la gorda – the fat one
se fue al – went to
llegó – arrived
ahora sólo quedas tú – now you're the only one left
tú sabes – you know
nalgas – buttocks
esas cosotas – those big things
pos, que se reventó el globo – well, the bubble burst
pos estaba viniendo – well, he was coming
una d'esas – one of those girls
cosa de viejas – women's stuff
cantina – bar
troquita – pick-up truck
quitó los zapatos – he took off his shoes
¡Ingrata! – Ingrate!
cabrona – the female form of "billy goat" or ass-hole – strong curse word for a
        person lacking manners and consideration
ya le calaba – it was already bugging him
que ya era tiempo – that it was high time already
y ya le andaban las moscas y el polvo – the flies and the dust were getting to him
hasta las 2:00 de la tarde, y lo único que vió – until 2 p.m., and all he saw

toallas – towels
sobras – scraps
calor – heat
amor de lejos – love at a distance
sin decirle nada – without saying anything to her
uno de los hombres que eran middle-aged y bien-respected – one of the middle-aged, well-respected men
y ella se portó bien también, nomás que – and she behaved herself well too, except that
y todo, qué desgracia, pero – and all, how shameful, but
cuídamelo – take care of him for me
y pataleando – and kicking
acompañarlo – be with him
m'ija 'ta más chula – my little girl is so cute
y ni le dieron – and they didn't even give him
suavecito – softly
hace mucho tiempo – it's been a long time
muy caballero – very gentlemanly
¡Ya para con estas tonterías! – Quit all this foolishness already!
soy una madre – I'm a mother
ya olvídate de esas cosas – just forget those things

Waiting Between the Trees

carne guisada – meat stew
comino – cumin seed
tímido – shy
vatos – guys
cariñoso – loving
molcajete – traditional Mexican mortar
duende – mischievous elf (in this case; there are multiple extended meanings)
fuera desperdicio – it would be a waste
¿Entiendes? – Do you understand?
tiendita – little store

Black Leather Lu

todo tiene remedio – every ill has a cure
telenovela – television soap opera

Tía

con mucho cariño – with much affection
vela – a votive candle
atole –a thick soup made of ground corn
una casita chiquita, calladita – a quiet, little house
sartenes – frying pans
frijol con queso – bean and cheese
caldo – soup

About the Author

Dr. Carmen Tafolla is the 2015 Poet Laureate of the State of Texas, the first Mexican-American to ever hold that post. She is the author of books of poetry, nonfiction works, and short stories for adults, as well as numerous books for children and young adults. She is among the most anthologized of all Latina writers. Her several books for children include *That's Not Fair! Emma Tenayuca's Struggle for Justice / ¡No Es Justo! La lucha de Emma Tenayuca por la justicia* (written with Sharyll Teneyuca), *Baby Coyote and the Old Woman / El Coyotito y la Viejita*, *What Can You DO With A Rebozo?*, *What Can You DO With A Paleta?* (an American Library Association "Notable Book" and the recipient of the 2010 Tomás Rivera Mexican American Children's Book Award) and *Fiesta Babies*.

Called a "world class writer" by Alex Haley, Tafolla's adult books include *Sonnets and Salsa*, a widely-praised collection of poetry now in its fourth printing, and the source of many of the texts she performs in her one-woman show, "My Heart Speaks a Different Language." This show has been performed throughout the U.S., and in England, Spain, Germany, Mexico, Canada, New Zealand, and Norway. Her dramatic talents make her performances both lively and of profound emotional impact. She is also the author of *Sonnets to Human Beings & Other Selected Works*, which includes not only the title selection (winner of the 1989 National Chicano Literature Contest), but a large selection of Tafolla's poems and short stories, as well as several essays on Tafolla and her work.

The Holy Tortilla and a Pot of Beans was originally intended for an adult readership, but its popularity among Latino teens resulted in it being nominated for, and eventually winning the 2009 Tomás Rivera Mexican American Book Award for Young Adult Literature.

Tafolla's poems and short stories are included in over 200 anthologies and in dozens of textbooks, at every level from elementary through university.

Born and raised in San Antonio, many of Tafolla's early poems employed the bilingual idiom of the city's westside. She has long been regarded as one of the masters of this type of poetic "code switching." *Curandera* (1983) is considered something of a core document in this regard. In the 1970s, Tafolla was the head writer for *Sonrisas*, a pioneering bilingual television show for children.

A scholar of note, Tafolla is the author of *To Split a Human: Mitos, Machos, y la Mujer Chicana, Recognizing the Silent Monster: Racism in the 90s*, and the delightful *Tamales, Comadres, & the Meaning of Civilization* (written with Dr. Ellen Riojas Clark), as well as numerous articles. Tafolla received her Ph.D. in Bilingual and Foreign Language Education from the University of Texas in 1982. She has held a variety of faculty and administrative posts at universities throughout the Southwest, including Associate Professor of Women's Studies at California State University at Fresno, and Special Assistant to the President for Cultural Diversity / Visiting Professor of Honors Literature at Northern Arizona University. She was the first Chicana to direct a Chicano Studies Center in the U.S. (Texas Lutheran College, 1973). She has been a freelance educational consultant on bilingual education, writing and creativity, and cultural diversity issues for over three decades. She currently holds a visiting professorship at the University of Texas at San Antonio.

Tafolla currently lives in the city of her ancestors, San Antonio, Texas, in a 100-year-old house called *Casa del Angel*, with her husband, Dr. Ernesto M. Bernal, her son and daughter, Carmen's mother, three cats, a dog, and a multitude of manuscripts, *molcajetes*, and books.

Among her many honors, one that she is particularly proud of is the 1999 Art of Peace Award, given by St. Mary's University for literature which contribute to "peace, justice, and human understanding."

For more information about Carmen Tafolla, selections from reviews written about her work, and contact information, please visit:

http://www.carmentafolla.com

Performances, interviews, biographical information and teacher resources are available at www.salsa.net

Acknowledgments

Profound appreciation to Bryce Milligan of Wings Press, for his dedication not only to this book, but to a long series of quality publications, bringing the heart and soul of South Texas to the world. And to Thelma Ortíz Muraida, whose artistic vision graces the cover, *mando con mucha admiración mis mil gracias*. The critical eye of the following individuals helped pull the manuscript into its final form: Ire'ne Lara Silva, Moisés Salvador Lara, Denise McVea, Velma Nanka-Bruce, and Roberto Bonazzi. In addition, each line and every voice in these stories has been echoed off the untiring ears of my best editor *y mi muy querido, la Voz de Tejas*, Dr. Ernesto M. Bernal. Lastly, I would like to thank my mother, my children, *y mis primos* for their patience while I mumbled about holy tortillas, precious dirt, and sacred pecans. – C.T.

Previous versions of the following stories have appeared in the journals and sources listed:

"The Pot Has Eyes" – *Texas Short Stories II*, ed. Billy Bob Hill & Laurie Champion (Dallas: Browder Springs Press, 2000).

"Tia" – *Fantasmas*, ed. Rob Johnson (Tempe, Arizona: Bilingual Press/ Editorial Bilingue; 2001).

"I Just Can't Bear It" – *Texas Short Stories*, ed. Billy Bob Hill (Dallas: Browder Springs Press, 1997).

"El Mojado No Existe" – *Sonnets to Human Beings and Other Selected Works by Carmen Tafolla*, ed. Ernesto Padilla (Santa Monica, California: Lalo Press, 1992).

"Chencho's Cow" – *Saguaro*, Vol. 4, ed. Miguel Mendez-M (Tucson: University of Arizona, 1987); *Common Bonds: Texas Women Writers* (Dallas: SMU Press, 1990); *Daughters of the Fifth Sun*, eds. Bryce Milligan, Mary Guerrero Milligan & Angela De Hoyos (New York: Riverhead Books, 1995); *Sonnets to Human Beings and Other Selected Works by Carmen Tafolla*, ed. Ernesto Padilla (Santa Monica California: Lalo Press, 1992).

"Federico Y Elfiria" – *Mosaic*, 1987; *Third Woman,*Vol. IV, 1989; *Sonnets to Human Beings and Other Selected Works by Carmen Tafolla*, ed. Ernesto Padilla (Santa Monica California: Lalo Press, 1992).

"How I Got Into Big Trouble and the Mistakes I Made, in Increasing Order of Importance" – *Red Boots & Attitude: The Spirit of Texas Women Writers*, eds. Diane Fanning & Susie Kelly Flatau (Austin:Eakin Press, 2002).

"La Santísima Maria Pilar, The Queen of Mean" – *TEX!* (Dallas: The Writers' Garret, 1998).

WINGS PRESS

Colophon

This third printing of *The Holy Tortilla and a Pot of Beans*, by Carmen Tafolla, has been printed on 60 pound Accent Opaque paper containing a percentage of recycled fiber. Titles have been set in Bremen and Harrington type, the text in Adobe Caslon type. All Wings Press books are designed and produced by Bryce Milligan.

On-line catalogue and ordering available at
www.wingspress.com

Wings Press titles are distributed to the trade by the
Independent Publishers Group
www.ipgbook.com
and in Europe by
www.gazellebookservices.co.uk